A DAY'S LOVING

A DAY'S LOVING

a novel
by

Hubert Gregg

BACHMAN & TURNER
LONDON

© Hubert Gregg 1974
First published 1974 by
Bachman & Turner
45 Calthorpe Street
London WC1X OHH

ISBN 085974 011 0

Printed by
W. & G. Baird Ltd
Antrim, Northern Ireland
and bound by
The Pitman Press Ltd, Bath

CHAPTER

1

The blue eyes of the railway porter/ticket clerk did nothing to offset the colour of his politics. These he wore not so much on his sleeve as all over him. And the little country station seemed ashamed. There was something about the quiet of Tagham that went ill with any thought of disturbance. And much about the porter/ticket clerk that boded nothing else but.

"Good morning. First class day return to London?" The clerk ignored the greeting. He fiddled with the small, modern ticket machine that was as much out of place in tranquillity as he was. Or is it we who are out of place Christopher wondered as he got his money ready. We who observe.

"Two pounds seventy five, that'll be". The blue ticket was proffered—there the colour was suitable—and the blue eyes did their best to pierce his. The eyes said "You want privilege, you pay for it". And added "It won't be long now". Christopher's own eyes met the challenge with a simple rejoinder. "Go and fuck yourself" they said.

He had come to live in Tagham only a few months ago. And though his train trips to London were restricted to one—at the outside two—per week, he had come to know this railway man. But he doubted whether the man knew him. He, Christopher, was an observer, a dreamer but one who saw. The clerk, a grinder without a sight to his blue eye or a dream to his didn't-matter-what name.

Christopher Tighson was going to matter. As a name. And the name was going to be sought after by those station kiosk fingers that sift the paper-backs. "A new Christopher Tighson!" an excited voice would be heard to say. One of these mornings. One book. One book, one film sale and a paper-back in consequence. So far. He had wasted precious years. Acting, or trying to then discovering others did it at least as well. Writing a play or two—one being produced at an out of London subsidised theatre. Somewhere along the wasted way he had met Jenny and married her. They had one child and he, Christopher, was on his way to London for his first taste of extra-marital sex relations.

He settled into a corner seat in a non-smoker. He liked the odd cigarette. But not more than he disliked company. The non-smoker tended to be empty all the way to London and, if you were alone, you could light up without being asked to leave the compartment. There were no ash trays, of course. He could never understand why. It could happen—as it would today—that a single traveller might smoke and then what? Or more than one, permission nicely asked. Before you can say "British Railway" you're up to your ankles in spent fags. Perhaps therein lay the answer, in those words BRITISH RAIL—the initials expensively woven into the carpets, the when-changed antimacassers. A non-smoker means a non-smoker, no matter what. If the train is jam full and your non-smoker is packed with tobacco addicts you MAY NOT SMOKE. By order of nationalised rail. Which was, supposedly, nationalised by and for you. "Balls" said Christopher, aloud, as he rose to re-tie his tie in the compartment glass.

He had to fold down his gangling height to do this, he was well over six feet. And not too flesh-covered. His face was starkly pale against the dark mop of his hair and the touch of feminine around the mouth said—in not more than a stage whisper—that this was not craggy-to-handsome so much as lean-to-pretty. Appealing, not too weak. But a powerful magnet to men. And the eyes—a more faded blue than the cornflower of the ticket clerk—didn't help. They had dark patches under them he saw, had had for some time. He ignored these and parted the too delicate lips to reveal large, white teeth—even and every one his own. "Not bad for thirty-nine" he said, aloud again, examining these in detail. ("Nine". Something of a gong sound about the word. One short of the gong.) "Not good either" he said back, allowing a glance at the dark patches. He was inclined to hold these dialogues in which both sides of a question were put, with stern justice. "Regular sex" he said, this time to himself, "That is what you lack". Aloud, he said "And that, from now on, is what you're going to get if you rupture yourself in the process".

His tie tied and his future thus, so to speak, put to bed, Christopher Tighson sat comfortably and withdrew from his brief case a springback cover that contained his second novel. This was why you travelled first class. A supplement for solitude. Did M.P.s set it against tax, did anyone with a professional need for spreading out papers? He caressed the white, imprisoned pages. Beautifully typed, he gave himself. On the leaf following the title, his two word dedication FOR JENNY. Yes. That was all right. No 'without whom this book would never have been . . . etc' crap. It wouldn't have been true anyway. More true to say 'in spite of whom and the yelling of that bloody baby . . . etc.'. That dedication, now that he came to admit it, was pure guilt. Like the flowers you bring home when you've cheated. He supposed. Being an observer. He had, as yet, never cheated but if you can cheat in thinking by God yes, he had. He turned the page. "My second". He had told something of the idea to Peter Grun, the film man who had bought his first. Not for a great deal of money, it was a good seller, not a best seller. And they carved the quality out of it on film. Peter Grun had wanted his second. But so did Murray's and Christopher had decided to see it in print. It might be a no-seller-at-all, in which case he would lose out, Peter would have cooled. But, then again . . . As he read, his mind went to Jenny . . .

9

"I'm Jenny Frühling".

"I know. They cast you for Caroline in Act Two".

"I love Act Two. In fact, I love Acts One and Two and that's not because they cast me as Caroline. This your first play?'

"Yes. It's taken me three years to get it on at Boughlea. Why 'Frühling'?"

"It's German. Means springtime".

It fitted like a shaft of sunlight. She was tallish as she stood and, he had to admit, all but skinny. Yet with a perfect little bosom that moved loosely and was, unchallengably, her own. The hair fell, in natural order, about her face, framing it with light. The colour was wheaty and he'd swear it had never known a dye bottle. The large eyes—grey, *very* large—had a surprised, awakening look that said they were seeing everything for the first time. 'Frühling' fitted.

"I knew. You're German, then?"

"My father was. Mother fraternised. They're both dead".

"Oh".

"Not because of. My grandmother was French and they went to visit her. The first holiday they'd ever had. Granny lived in Frejus".

"Not . . . ?'

"The floods. Yes".

"I'm sorry".

"It's long, long ago".

She perched on the upturned seat beside him and waited for him to speak.

"I think you'll be good as Caroline, I saw your audition."

"I love the part. And it isn't too big, thank God".

"Why?"

"If it's a big part you never get to play it in London. On the transfer".

"You think it will? Transfer?'

She plopped down the seat and sat, considering.

"It's good. And not too preachy, that may be one reason for not. Transferring. But they do transfer from here. They

10

don't work too hard at getting the managements down, they're a bit snobby, being subsidised".

"You're cheering me up no end. Shall we go for coffee?"

"Thanks but I have to get off to a fitting. You coming to all the rehearsals?'

"You think I shouldnt?'

"I think you might ache a bit, seeing all the things that happen to something you've created. Like having a baby then watching the hospital staff play football with it. I'd like to see you again, though. Is that forward?"

"It's nice".

"Maybe tomorrow when we plot Act Two?'

"Maybe".

'Maybe' was 'Yes' and after Act Two came a meal. A meagre one, topped off with coffee at his cheap hotel. Jenny was in digs.

As the days passed, he became drawn to her innocence, her candour. And her body.

The play was well received but no London management came and only the *Stage* critic. (The five most useless things in life, he had learned from the Character Man, are a man's tits, the Pope's balls and a good notice in The Stage.) 'A promising entry into the writing side . . .' they said, they had noticed that he had been, still was, an actor. 'Jenny Frühling was a forthright Caroline . . .', what the hell did that mean? Sounded like a pregnant belly with a corn-flower stuck in it. The play didn't sell.

On the last night, the theatre subsidy ran to beer and sandwiches. Commiseration, congratulation—the latter the stronger. The Boughlea Everyman Theatre never admitted a mistake. "Don't forget to let us have your next one, Chris".

They were seated, knees up, on the floor of the stalls bar. He put aside the sausage roll and asked her . . .

"Where do you live in London?"

"I have a room off the Cromwell Road, where do you?"

"I have a flat. Sort of. I share it with an actor but he's away on tour a lot".

"Like now?"

11

"Like now. May I telephone you?"

"You may but you can't, I'll telephone you. It's in the hall, I mean, and it doesn't always work and the ear-piece is sticky".

"Who uses it? Apart from you?"

"Immigrants. And three secretaries from the Ministry of Power, they're the ones who make the ear-piece sticky".

"What do you live on?'

"What kind of a question is that? Out of the blue?"

"Just a question out of the blue, I'm sorry. No I'm not, I want to know".

"I did a T.V. commercial for a choc bar".

"You didn't! They're disgusting".

"I found out. You've gone all red. Anyway, it still brings in residuals. I manage. What do *you* live on?"

"Christ knows. I've written bits and pieces, like radio plays. With parts for me. When I get it I put it away. What I can. Let's travel up together, shall we? To London?'

"Wish you'd said that yesterday".

"I didn't think of it yesterday, why?"

"I said I'd drive up with Mark. Tonight".

"Mark? What's with Mark?"

"Nothing. Except a clapped-out Triumph with a leak in the back axle".

"Tell him you'll go tomorrow. By train".

"I can't. I have nowhere to sleep, I gave up my digs".

Christopher lapped at his warm beer and peered across the theatre bar to where Mark—who had bitched up one of the leads in his play—was having his thigh felt by the director.

"I didn't know he was queer" he said.

"He isn't. Just ambitious".

"How old are you, Jenny Springtime?"

"Nineteen, aren't I advanced?'

"Yes".

"How old are you?"

"Guess".

"That means you're wondering if you look as old as you are. And that means you wish you weren't. Twenty-nine? Thirty?"

"That'll do".

12

"That means thirty-one?"

'Yes. I'm ahead by twelve years".

"So, who cares?"

"I could get you a room at my hotel"

"Ooh. No strings, you mean?"

"No strings".

"No strings but who pays, I can't?"

"I can".

"You can but you may'nt, I won't be anybody's kept woman".

"Kept women render service, you don't have to render a thing. You can pay me back if you like. Out of your next residual".

"Should I argue any more?"

"You've argued enough for a good girl, you may now surrender".

"To one night's keep, returnable?"

"Yes".

"I'll tell Mark".

Jenny remained intacta that night but it wasn't going to be long.

CHAPTER

2

The train stopped at the little station Christopher could never remember the name of. A painful halt always because the four carriages now had to have a sizeable train yoked to them so that it became pukkah main line London. Again, today, the yoking jolted his spine. It shot the spring-back out of his hand too, and the beautifully typed pages out of the spring-back.

"Fuck" he said aloud.

A tweedy lady paused in the doorway to look astonished. She decided not to enter and Christopher jack-knifed down

13

to scratch about on the filthy carpet amassing his so clean pages. Two more jolts banged his head and grazed his elbow but he was dogged. As the train drew away from whatever-its-name-was he sat again, putting the spring-back, newly arranged, on the seat beside him. He rose and, again, peered at his face in the glass. "You've gone all red" a voice seemed to say. And he remembered the first time that Jenny had gone all red . . .

"A whole flat, all to yourself. How does it feel?" she said, continuing to explore.

"It's only half a whole flat".

"You said he's on tour".

"He'll be back".

"You must write another play and it will sell for a film if you put lots of naked ladies in it . . .

"Naked men might bring in more".

"Naked men, then. And you can have two whole flats, one for me".

"That would make you a kept woman".

"Not if I pay the rent it wouldn't".

"And where are you going to get the money, you can't go on sucking that bloody bar for ever".

"I shall appear in your new play. Write me a tidgy-widgy part and I might even get it in the film".

"A naked part?"

"No, I don't think I'd like a naked part. I wouldn't mind a quick scene but it wouldn't be like that, would it? Sandy Smale did it and she said never again".

"Who's Sandy Smale?"

"A highly sexy friend of mine. She looks super in the nude and she spends a lot of time in it but even she jibbed".

"What at?"

"All those technicians. And she had to do her own stand-ing-in. Hours it took while they got the lights right on her . . . You know".

"Poor Sandy".

"And then this awful young man got into bed with her right in front of everybody".

14

"Part of the plot?"

"Oh yes. But he kept his Y-fronts on, it was all right for him. She had to strip to the buff because her hip was in shot or something and he pressed himself all over her top".

"I think I'll stick to naked men in my play, they don't have tops. Can you cook?"

'What kind of a question is that? No".

"I can a bit. Shall I make us some scrambled eggs?"

"I can cook scrambled eggs, I thought you meant the cordon bleu bit. Where's the kitchen?"

He had had the odd female in the flat before, of course, but Jenny did something more than give it a whiff of scent. She fascinated him. Like a Tinker Bell light. She flitted like it and was as difficult to pin down.

"You've lived a lot for nineteen" he called out. When she answered from the kitchen her raised voice was marvellously young and clear.

"Because I have a sexy girl friend? It's a bit second hand".

"You sound sorry".

"I'm in no hurry. When it comes it comes and it'll be super. Just so long as it isn't crummy".

"What do you mean?"

She didn't answer and he repeated the question. He could hear the sound of eggs being cracked and plopped.

"I'm not being corny, really, but I think I'd like to be in love. Or at least I'd like to have my breath taken away. Then it wouldn't be crummy".

"I see".

After more cracking and plopping . . .

"Shall I use the last egg or do you want it for breakfast?"

"How many have you got so far?"

"Four. Shall I use five?"

"Five".

There was a pause, then a crack and a plop. Then she said . . .

"Fuck".

"Jenny!"

15

She appeared in the doorway and Tinker Bell had gone all red.

"I didn't mean it".

"What do you mean you didn't mean it?"

"What I said. It slipped out because the fifth egg was bad and I didn't break it into a cup first".

"Then you chose just the word. I use it myself, quite often".

"Well, I don't and I did and I shouldn't have". She looked so forlorn he had to take her in his arms. Tenderly, because she was the most crushable thing he'd ever held.

After such a first physical encounter he was accustomed to progress at speed. But not with Jenny. She was a new kind of intriguing package and he wanted to delay opening. Indeed, he had the strange feeling that he would put this package on a near shelf and contemplate it for some long time to come. Even, never opening. This was madness. But it was new too, everything about Jenny was new. As though she had the power to give her awakening eyes to others that they might begin again at April and have no wish to hurry on to July. July comes all too soon. He lifted her face and kissed a tear that was on its way down.

"There's an old film on at the Classic round the corner" he said. "Clark Gable for you, Claudette Colbert for me".

They saw *It Happened One Night* and ate at a nearby café, holding hands under the table. There was candle-light, of all surprising things, and he studied her by its flattery. This kind of creature you kept close. You cherished and were careful not to damage. Like a bird in hand. The feel of the down on your fingers, the frightened heart beating. The settling and trusting. How did you possess springtime?

They met at near intervals, Jenny got a small part in Television . . .

"Not a naked part, no. I was offered a bath soap commercial and I turned it down, did I tell you?"

"Lots of residuals".

16

"You don't live by residuals alone. It says in the Bible".

"Does it, now?"

"This part is a delinquent. Hard as nails and old as Father Time but not so wise".

"Who says Time is wise? Who says he doesn't get sillier the longer gets his beard?"

"You're a cynic. How's the play coming?"

"How did you know I'm writing?"

"Because you never talk about it and because your flat is bunchy with typescript. When is Jason coming back from tour?'

"Next week. It's a novel this time. I didn't talk about it because it may not get born".

"When are you due?"

"I'm already in labour—the first stage".

"What does that mean? How many stages are there to labour?'

"Three".

"And how do you know then, and not me? I'm the one who'll have to do it all one day".

"Not with a novel. Anyone can have a baby, it's nature. It's against nature to write so much down. You're stripping a part of you to its socks and it can be very stare-causing. I knew a medical student" he said, answering her at last.

"So anyone can have a baby?"

"It isn't difficult".

It wasn't. As the train screeched to a standstill some-where in Sussex, he was reminded how easy it had been.

He had been present at the birth—Jenny insisted—but he knew all along it would be a mistake. At the age of eight, he had watched kittens being born and had been sick all day. Yet, with the sometimes stubborn refusal of the young to connect A with B, he had passed to later years without ever, for a moment, thinking that a human did it like that. The eight months ago, middle-of-the-night nearness and the contemplation and the "Just think, someone who will

17

B

be made up of both of us!"—God, how many times, how many corny ways had that been said!—became, at last, the clinical stretch-out on the bare bed, the *same* bed. The fairy tale explanations thought up by Victorians. They had their reason. The desperation in humans to shut away the basic functions of the nether end.

It didn't look like an apoplectic Peke, that was a relief. But the head was elongated, like those of some African natives who work at it for beauty. It was damned near as long as the body. The midwife—or whatever the doctor's helper was called—swaddled the new being, turbanning the head so that nothing could be seen above the forehead.

"A good thing I induced" said the doctor. "Even so, there was a good deal of moulding. Don't worry about the head, it will be normal within a matter of days".

Later the nurse added "Wonderful how nature can mould the bones of the skull to let the child through . . ."

It—he couldn't think of the baby as 'he'—was like a china doll, delicately coloured. Not boiled-looking at all. 'Moulding,' 'induced'? To Christopher it had seemed simple. He had not been conscious of the agony in Jenny as she held his hand. As the long head began to emerge, the terror was his alone, that he, Christopher Tighson could produce a monster. Bewilderment at the smile on the face of the doctor, the complacent efficiency of the nurse. His monster held aloft like a skinned rabbit. This was the object that had so disfigured his Jenny, pushing out from inside that slim girl until she became a grotesque. "I want her to bear this child a month, at least, ahead of time" the doctor had said. "She's a healthy girl. Take her to Hampstead Heath and run her about". Lunatic dashes over the humps, they had made, the passers-by amazed. That—and the injections —had forced the monster to make his early entry into the bedroom. "Don't worry about the head . . ."

There followed a three week small Bedlam. The nurse took over the house, he had expected it. It was like one of those newspaper games where they draw a maze and the trick is for you, on the outside, to reach the rich, innermost point of the labyrinth and you get your marks. He was on the outside. The nurse and Rex—that was his king of a

18

name—were the lines that led here, there, nowhere. At the heart of the maze was Jenny. Unattainable. Not wanting to be attained.

He had to watch the nurse dealing with the child, bathing it, drying it, powdering its raw little genitals. Ankles both held in a firm hand, the wriggling life upended, turned over, turned back. And parcelled up—June and a heat wave, the poor bugger must be sweltering in there. The package delivered to Jenny in another room where she fed her milk to it. What will happen to that perfect bosom?'

Christopher, of course, gave it a bath. Day by day, it became to him more of a small, knowing animal whose increasing prowess he was expected to admire. At three weeks, he was present as the nurse held the baby up in the bath, the tiny feet just touching the bottom.

"Watch" she said and he couldn't do anything but. The feet began to stab at the bath and fought to make forward progress.

"He's walking!"

"Hardly, but it's the natural instinct. Fascinating, isn't it?"

He began to tire of the novelties. One day, holding this 'someone made up of both of them', he wondered idly whether Rex would grow up to have anything of either. Money, he would cost. More and more money until one day, paradoxically—continuing to eat up the money, he would begin to feel independent and express the feeling. Finally, having consumed his full banquet of Exchequor, he would rise from the board, chew up enough saliva to spit in both their faces and turn his rear to them, farting as he made the exit, and there would be one more paid-up member of the People. Family ties (laughter), birthdays with the key of the door at majority (more laughter), the loyalties . . . Christopher was just old enough to remember these and not young enough to sneer . . . The sitting down, replete, at Christmas to hear the Queen's speech—on the wireless (loud, prolonged laughter) . . . She must be hard put to it to think of something to say at Christmas now, poor woman. It's a P.V.C. world, a coward, new world in which the love bed is a whoring-couch. A world that laughs off the top of its head and never from the belly. A world not up to believing that which is not laid bare to it. A world of smart Alecs who know all the answers, hide nothing, tell all. To which Jenny and I have contributed one more smart Alec named Rex.

Jenny had to exercise. To reduce the bag of jelly that her young stomach had become and to call back the breasts he needed.

They moved loosely under her cotton dress as she laid the table.

"What are we having?"

"Chicken special. Carrier's. With a little something of my own to follow".

Huge, grey eyes looked up at him and the thin face had the makings of a blush. They hadn't yet reached the stage of laughing at two meanings. She saw them, he was sure, but the relationship was too young for sharing. You didn't share except with a lover and even then you were wary of puncturing too many balloons. They would be lovers, he knew. But, over the weeks, he had savoured the progress, not eager to lose whatever it was he sensed would vanish forever. To be followed by . . . ?Something different. She was a virgin, of that he was in no doubt. And the ripening of their story was, in itself, precious to him—a pleasure she couldn't know. The plucking of the fruit would bring its own sadness. In the very joy of it.

There was a deeper reason for his delay.

She returned to the kitchen and he flopped into a near-springless armchair covered with cretonne of now uncertain design. He gathered up a heap of typed pages from the self at his elbow. The novel was complete. Except for the polishing he had come not to mind. The pruning, even, gave satisfaction to his liking for order. As long as they

20

didn't ask him to rewrite. They, who? A publisher would be found then, prepared to print down his dream? He had no doubt that one would, with the supreme confidence of the first-novel writer he was well pleased with this, his beloved son. It didn't enter the mind that the child might not find acceptance. But how if they liked not the whole baby? "Rewrite chapters one to forty and let us see it again". You would lop off an arm, a leg and run up new ones, stick them to the body using a brand new pot of dreamers' glue—no guarantee of exact standard, the quality may vary . . .

Out of the compartment window Christopher read, painted along a wall LOOK TO YOUR SOUL and it put him off consideration of his own writing until they reached Arundel.

Look to your soul, look to the words you put down. Spill your soul or portion it out, not even your soul, judging the market value. He wanted this novel to sell. But which was the greater want, the selling want or the want to say part of him?

"Won't be long" she called from the kitchen.

"No hurry".

Christopher had gone cold. Ludicrously, he saw himself, fifty years from now, asking in a public library "I'm looking for the first Christopher Tighson, 'Some Defect In Her' is the title . . . ".Would he ask with pride, would the book be there, even? If the two answers were 'No', burn it now. And peddle toys on the street corner for money. Whom do you deceive? Which part of your integrity do you lay bare . . . when you write because you want to marry Jenny? There are no parts to integrity. There is or there isn't. He whipped page after page over savagely as though to beat intent into the writing on them.

"What's this bottle?"

"What bottle?"

"In the freezer. It's champagne! What are we celebrating?"

21

"The fact" said he, only to himself, "that, since Jason returns tomorrow, I am about to deflower you, peel off your innocence, share two meanings".

"Just . . . our last dinner here alone. Until Jason goes on tour again, at all events . . . Do you mind champagne?"

There was a pause before her answer that drove a stupid knife into him. Her answer drove it deeper.

"I've never had champagne".

"Jenny! Never?"

"Don't I sound like a poor little waif? Never. Do *you* mind? I'll get squiffy".

"No you won't, I won't let you. Get squiffy on your first taste of champagne? An insult to the grape".

He had known. Or sensed that champagne might be new. And in consequence there was, of course, the possibility . . . Christ, this was like all the rest. The ingrained technique taking over, once you acquired it it was damned difficult to drop. Get her a little the worse. The music and the cheek against hers in dancing . . . Dear God, no, not with Jenny. His precious package, can't we forget technique tonight and *behave*? Behaviour was a very poverty-stricken brother when technique came slumming. He put down the manuscript and went quietly to the door of the kitchen.

"Hullo, Jenny Springtime".

"Hullo" she said.

Her face had a culinary glow now and her saucer eyes saw right into him. And what they saw was good, wasn't it, you couldn't deceive Jenny? He did love her, he did love her.

They touched glasses and Jenny tasted the grape in all its sophistication.

"M'm".

"Like?"

She wrinkled her nose at the first encounter with these bubbles. "Like" she said.

The meal wasn't bad. There would have been an intake of breath from Carrier but he wasn't there. Christopher

22

poured again for them, then put the bottle aside. The gesture was wasted on Jenny.

"Like my dinner?"

"Liked. I didn't leave a morsel".

He would not have added for the world that, as an evacuee kid, he had had it early bred into him to leave nothing, but nothing, on the plate. He had enjoyed it, though. His thirty-one-year-old heart now beating like mad, there was one in the eye for technique. Yes. The first time it had too, but that was young nature. The second time not much, the third not at all. Now, for Jenny . . . One decision he had made firmly, he would not play music. If the mood needed helping he would leave the mood alone and tonight would be one more of many. No music.

"Put on some music".

Well, All right then, this was an outside decision, not his.

"Bach?" he did try.

"Baccarach".

'Anyone who had a heart', one of Jason's, he plopped on to the player. And Jenny, her eyes tilting to him in expectation of displeasure, poured herself another glass of the grape. Let that go, too.

He adored her legs that were long and scrawny. Straight, beautifully straight. If she were famous you wouldn't insure them for a million, he supposed, but they were gorgeous Jenny. He noticed them now because she rose and drank from her glass in a ridiculous, reach-up position. The legs—and the tights—seemed to go on, up and up, forever. His first girl sleepers had worn stockings. With suspenders and the wonderful, soft skin gap between stocking top and pant. Pant? There is no singular of pants and some girls say 'panties' because it's supposed to be more feminine. Christopher had news for the supposers. 'Pant', no, but 'pants' yes, 'pants'. Stronger and sexier by far than 'panties' which sound as though it isn't quite the thing that they should be taken down. He sorrowed for suspenders and their passing. Jenny's were the first tights he had approved of. So far. Because, he said to Christopher, they went on up and up forever.

23

"Some Defect In Her' . . . That's a quotation, isn't it?"

"Yes. The Tempest".

"You played Ferdinand, I saw the picture in your cutting book".

"Who said you might look at my cutting book?"

"Were you good?"

"Nobody can be good as Ferdinand. Some poor, bloody actor has to play him, though. At the Open Air, Regent's Park it was me".

"Did it rain?"

"Not often enough".

"What's the rest of it? The quotation?"

"Oh God, I don't remember. 'Many a woman have I liked . . .' . . . or something . . . no . . . 'For several virtues have I liked several women . . . Never any with so full soul . . .' "

Look to your soul . . .

"Go on".

". . . with so full soul but some defect in her . . . did quarrel with the noblest grace she owed and put it to the sword . . ."

"He was a bit choosy, Ferdinand".

'I can't think what Miranda saw in him. Except that what were the alternatives? Caliban—a monster—and Ariel—a poof. And all that stuff he says to his prospective father-in-law . . ."

"Old Prospero?"

"Old Prospero. When he tells Ferdinand to watch it and not bed his daughter down before the nuptials . . ."

"What does he say? Ferdinand?"

"Er . . . Don't you know? You won't believe it if you don't and I had to say it with a straight face . . ."

"What?'

" 'The white cold virgin snow upon my heart . . . abates the ardour of my liver".

"You're not serious".

"I am and so was he. Except that I don't think he had a liver".

But she had thrown back her head and was rocking with

the youngest laughter he had ever heard. The champagne in her glass rocked too and she said "Whoops".

Baccarach came to an end. Christopher put down his own glass and turned off the record player. Then he went to Jenny and took her glass away and held her in his arms as he had done on that first night here. Her face was warm and she smelled of newly baked biscuits. No scent at all, technique would have been put out as Hell. But it was nowhere to be felt. There was just Jenny and they were close. He brought the champagne glass from behind her back, round and up to before her lips and she sipped, he sipping too, on the backward tilt. Then he held the glass while she took in the last, small helping of the grape. At once, he kissed her. As her lips parted he tasted the grape too. She spluttered.

"I say, that's a bit forward. You pinched my champers".

"I don't want you to get squiffy".

"Why?"

They were forehead to forehead and the room was full of her eyes.

"Isn't that what you do to all your women, lure them up here and get them squiffy and then whoops?"

"All, without exception".

"Exception me".

"Come again?"

"I said excepting me".

"You didn't. You may have thought you did but you didn't".

"Do you mind if we sit down?"

He moved away, taking her hand, but she drew him back to her.

"Don't leave . . . Let's go together".

As they walked to the beat-up sofa . . . scene of so many a technique triumph . . .

"So you've liked many women?"

They walked head to head but he made no answers. She pursued it . . .

"Never any and so on . . . but some defect in her . . . Is it your story then, your novel, is that why you won't let me read it?"

25

"No fear. And you can read it if you like. Only . . ."

"Only?"

They settled back and one sofa spring twanged a protest.

"It isn't that I mind criticism . . ."

"Yes? But?"

"I just couldn't rewrite. Any of it. It either is or it isn't. So if you said you didn't like this bit or that bit . . . don't be offended . . . but it couldn't make any difference, I can't rewrite".

"You mean I say I like it or I don't like it, no dissecting?"

"No dissecting. Want to take it home with you tonight?"

"Am I going home tonight?" She said it with no art at all. Technique should be prepared for whatever surprise, he tried to call it back but couldn't.

"You said exception me".

"I know I did. But I've wanted to so much and you did and you didn't. I liked that".

"I did and I didn't?"

"So, it's routine, so what?"

"It isn't . . . quite routine".

"I bet you don't always get in champagne though, I bet that's a bit special. Isn't it?"

"Absolute, first time special".

They held each other very close for a long, quiet while. Into his tie, she said . . .

"I wonder . . . what defect in me will quarrel with the noblest grace I have . . . Or perhaps I haven't got graces?"

"You've got your own, who wants Grace's?"

They laughed until the spring twanged again and then they laughed at that. Cheaply, he had overstepped the non-share barrier. She had too, she was laughing . . . But he held her more closely.

"Did you want coffee?" she ventured.

"No, I didn't. That's if you didn't, I didn't. Did you?"

"Only if you did".

"Isn't 'did' a silly word?"

"It's foreign. It isn't English at all, it's foreign".

"The Dids attacked at first light . . ." he said.

26

She laughed and her two hands came together like a child applauding. He played up to her.

". . . but the Shoulds outdid them . . ."

"The Shoulds outdid . . ." She laughed and clapped, then, all at once, she was silent and hid against him.

"Why are we pretending we're squiffy when we're not?" she asked suddenly. "Is it because we're afraid we might say something we really mean?" She had drawn away and her eyes were searching his.

"You haven't kissed me" she accused. "Ever".

"I have too. I pinched your champers".

"Slick. That was a slick little kiss, you got one in when I wasn't ready. That wasn't a kiss."

The short range scrutiny would have made him pull away but she held his head firmly, within inches of hers.

"This is a kiss" she announced, as though to herself or to an unseen voyeur, not to him.

Soft, her lips, and they parted almost as in surprise. Then her tongue, a shy, exploring infant, penetrated, stopped, explored again. She gave a little cry as their tongues met and her head worried gently from side to side as though she were shaking it for "No". He did not take over the kiss, it was hers alone. At last, she drew away and looked at him again, the headlamp eyes leaving no hiding place within Christopher.

"That's a kiss" she announced again, quietly. And he knew for certain that she had never kissed in quite that way before.

CHAPTER

4

One more stop and this time the train filled, it seemed, with schoolboys. Screaming, stamping horrors, half grown up Rexes with little men faces, lifeless hair. And smelling of egg and urine. One or two were pretty. With baby's bum cheeks and peach fuzz and inch-long eyelashes, why did Nature do that? He, Christopher, had been such a one. He turned to his manuscript but he couldn't get the picture out of his mind.

"Not playing today?"

Young Chris looked up from his Bell's Concise Latin and saw the sub-prefect. His senior only by virtue of the band round his cap. When he wore it. At this moment, his head was a mop of disordered, blond curls. He was good looking but with too strong a jaw. His jet black eyes were startling in a head with such hair to crown it.

"I hurt my wrist".

Through the classroom window came the whack of a square hit cricket ball and a bee buzzed near the desk. "So you're getting up Latin?"

"Next to maths it's my weakest subject. I need it for a pass".

St. Michael's was a small country college that clung to the hem of the Public School list. But for Mr. and Mrs. Templar, his foster parents in evacuation, he would never have made it this high. His own father, a careful Civil Servant, hated his job, put up for every Board that was going, lived only for the petty promotions and the consequent ratcheting up of his salary to jack the pension that would keep tidy the late years. He said yes and yes and yes—or, more exactly, never said no. And took his reward. Christopher's mother had brought in a little money, his father had married carefully. Not much money, that would have called for, in his father, a spirit of daring that could never be his. Marry too well and you're in trouble, marry a little money. The little, optimistically invested, was halved by the post war Labour landslide. Tighson Senior's overweaning confidence in gilt-edged helped not at all. For the remainder of her ailing life, his mother could barely afford the paints and canvasses that were her private ladder to the sky. She died before that dear Mr. Churchill came back and her husband entered retirement alone.

The Templars had become too attached to young Chris to want to let go completely. He had done well at his prep. school, paid for by them, and there was this very good little college only twelve miles away. He didn't have to board. And the Templars would pay—it would be their return to the Tighsons for the joy their Chris had brought to a childless couple . . . was the way they put it. Tighson Senior had said yes.

"My tour of duty is just over, that's why I'm not playing. Care to come to my room? I've just got my whole month's chocolate ration, we can scoff the lot if you like".

Christopher was permanently peckish. He was conscious that the Templars had always directed the lion's portion of their meagre rations to him and, sensitive kid though he was, he made no demur. The Battle of the Atlantic couldn't have been expected to mean a thing in his young life. Nor, now that the war was over, could he appreciate that the winners would be worse off than the losers. It seemed to him, merely, that no matter how much food—in quantity— you ate you were hungry again within half an hour.

"A month's ration?" No more attractive bait could have swung his way.

They were sprawled on the bed, eating. Christopher's eyes on the ceiling above, he oblivious of the sly approach on his left. The sub-prefect, chatting, eating, laughing, was now very close and—apparently to emphasise something he was saying—clapped a hand on Christopher's thigh. For a moment he gave it no thought, it seemed a natural gesture, like an arm round the shoulder. But the hand stayed. It slid to Christopher's groin and he froze.

"Relax. What are you so tensed up for?" The hand was caressing now and, to Christopher's horror, his penis began to harden.

"You can't pretend you don't like it, can you?" leered the voice. "Why don't you touch me?" Christopher wanted to shout, to leap up. But he continued to harden and his head began to swim.

No more than a week ago he had known this hardness for the first time. Half waking, half asleep, he had felt the warm wetness, the exquisite release. Fully awake, exploring, he had been overjoyed at the evidence of manhood. Now, he was paralysed with the horror.

"Touch me".

He groped slowly to his left, found the groin and the parts there and grabbed, pressed. The sub-prefect yelped like a dog, shot off the bed and serve him bloody well right. Only now did he realise that he had used his damaged hand and it hurt like hell but he was half way through the door.

"Christ! You little bastard". The sub-prefect, bent double, was spewing his chocolate on to the floor. To the retreating figure he said, controlling the shout . . . "I'll get you. See if I don't. Christ".

Next day, as Christopher was showering after fives he heard lowered voices in the changing-room. A warning light flashed in his young mind. He reached for his towel and wrapped it firmly round his middle. There was no way out, the showers led off the changing-room and his clothes hung there. He paused for a moment, shivering, he didn't dare remove the towel to dry himself. The voices were raised now and there was laughter. Someone subdued it and a silence followed. Slowly, he pushed open the door. The sub-prefect was there with four minions and they stood in solemn contemplation of him.

"Hullo, young Tighson" said the sub-prefect.

'Hullo" he said and moved to get his shirt. His way was barred.

"What's the hurry? You're very nice as you are, isn't he?" The minions sniggered, only one looking uncomfortable.

"I'm cold".

"He's cold".

They sniggered again, all but one. The one said "Let him go, he's just played a bloody good game of fives".

"Has he, now?"

"I'm cold".

"So he's good at ball games, is he, I must say it's news to me".

The black eyes scanned him up and down. Like the dart of a snake's tongue, an arm came out and the towel was

30

ripped away. Christopher made a dive for his clothes but was pinned at once by three of the four. They swung him to a sitting position on a bench, one behind locking his arms, the others grabbing each a leg.

"Easy, now" said the sub-prefect.

"He's big for his age, isn't he?" slobbered the fat boy who held his right leg.

"Very" said the school scrum-half, at his left.

"I think we ought to let him go, he'll catch his death" said the dissenter.

"Shut up, Weasel" said the powerful boy holding his arms.

"He gets bigger if you give him encouragement" said the sub-prefect, advancing. Christopher made a giant effort to kick himself free and his left knee cracked the scrum-half on the jaw.

"Shit!"

Christopher shouted with pain as the angered boy put an arm over the knee joint and came back heavily on to it with the side of his body.

"You'll break his leg, you fool!"

"He won't try that again. Look, Weasel, shut up or go home".

"Yes".

"You're spoiling the fun".

"Not much fun".

"You haven't seen what I've seen" said the sub-prefect. "Mind you, he doesn't appreciate it. Pull him forward a bit. There". To Christopher he said, kneeling now . . . "These weren't made for rough treatment, you know. This is the way . . ." Christopher's eyes widened with apprehension, his whole body strained but was held.

"This is the way . . ." The soft hand began to caress and he gave a loud, retching cry.

"See what I mean? He doesn't appreciate it one little bit and I'm an expert". The hand continued to knead gently and Christopher jerked his head back against the strong chest behind him. He turned, tried to hide his face. The worse horror began.

"There, now. He likes it, doesn't he? Much bigger, didn't I tell you?"

Some of his shame seemed to pass to the minions for they relaxed their hold. Christopher made a leap for the door. The sub-prefect anticipated, would have barred his way. But the dissenter shouldered him as the other three recovered and, pushing the naked boy through into the corridor, turned to face the four. There was no pursuit. Only laughter followed him on his panic way down the long, covered passage that led to the lavatories. Quieter, the laughter, as he turned the corner, no pursuit. He crashed through a door into one of the cubicles, slammed it shut and locked it and, flinging himself down on to the wooden seat, began to sob.

An hour later, Christopher emerged into a silence that seemed to echo. No more fun this day.

No deep mark was left on him. He finished his schooling at another establishment—beyond the first, obvious inquiry his foster parents had asked nothing, had even moved house to be near him again. Why was it that foster-parents were always closer to what parents should perhaps be? They had staked him half way through university where he read English and History. While at Oxford, he had written sketches for the O.U.D.S. and had played in them and this gave him an urge to act professionally. Writing on the side, writers must always write on the side. Unless patronised. The patronage of the Templars was not enough and, in any event, could not be allowed to continue. His mother was ailing, his father coming up to retirement. The Templars would have mortgaged their souls but for God's sake they had done enough. He left Oxford, won a scholarship to a small Drama School in South Kensington which even carried a grant, we were on our way.

No deep mark. But, if undergraduate boastings were to be listened to, he was a late starter. It was at Drama School, only, that he had his first physical relations with a girl. He had none of the usual young trouble over holding back for her satisfaction. And he reached his own climax. But he discovered that the stimulation was not as strong at the second meeting. By the third he was bored and was constrained to make a new conquest. Then another, no girl could continue to excite him over a period of more than weeks. He gained, among the students, a reputation for promiscuity and this made them wary. He took to pursuing the innocents. And he discovered a new stimulation in the fact that he was awakening eager senses for the first time.

Sixteen, she was.

"I've never done this before".

"Of course".

"You haven't said you love me".

". . . No".

"You do, don't you, because if you don't then I shouldn't be here". Oh, Christ. But she was taking off her dress.

"Look. 'Love' is a word I never use, I don't think I can ever be in love". This was a line he would find to be infallible later. It evoked immediate sympathy. And any girl, he was to learn, to whom you said this at once set out to prove that she alone could break the monotony.

"You're wicked".

"Ah yes. I am". Spoken with a hint of sadness and of longing to be different?

"And I'm wicked too, I must be". Reassure her?

"There's something of the wicked in all of us". And off came the dress.

Unlike the others she had not retired to the bathroom to do whatever it is they do there. Among other things, he supposed, to top and tail. She hadn't and he was fastidious but you couldn't take exception. She smelled of baby soap and her body was quite beautiful. The schoolgirlish bra didn't fit, she bulged over it, and the tiny pants didn't match and bore a large, neat repair. They lay on the bed and, in the half light that came from the sides of the pulled down blind, he caressed her. His hand cupped her pudendum and it was like holding a peach. She arched her body. The sudden, first awareness, the thrill to her, became a thrill to him. He kissed her and her lips parted, mechanically, as though she knew they should. And the tongue acted according to the wicked book. Suddenly, the senses took over unguided and she gave a little moan of discovery.

The tiny pants had been slid away. Kissing her, he began to undo her bra. Her hands grasped his firmly and she

33

pulled away from the kiss looking with frightened eyes. "Nobody's ever seen me. Naked".

"Of course". He tried again and succeeded in undoing the hooks. But, as he slipped the straps down, he saw tears in her eyes.

"What is it?"

"Are you sure you love me?"

"I never said I did. In fact, I said I didn't, we agreed we're wicked". She moaned again.

"Would you like me to take you home?"

For answer, she drew him to her and clung. Kissing the side of his face. "You will be careful?"

"I promise".

"Nobody's ever . . .I haven't . . .and you don't . . ." He kissed the protest from her lips but, as he loosened the bra and took it away, she covered her breasts with arms and hands. My God, what was this? He should be bored to Hell with this simpleton but he had never known such desire. He got up and began to take off his shirt. She peered at him, wondering, like a child watching a conjuror about to do a trick. Some trick, how his earlier, experienced girls would laugh!

He stood in his underpants, uncertain how to take the next fence. Her shameless eyes fixed on him mid-way, her arms and hands prudishly covering. He went to stand above her on the bed, leant over her, his clenched hands on either side of her supporting him. He knelt astride her, took the hands in his and wrenched them apart and above her head so that there was no more concealing. Her large breasts were there, for the first time, to see.

It was a special excitement teaching them. And the book of your own technique grew to volumes. But the day always came that brought the onset of boredom. And the weeks that led to it were weeks in which their affection wrapped itself round you like a weed. Rooting it out roughed up the technique and there was always "what now?" It was no pleasant task working up to a deflowering.

5

Christopher laid aside his manuscript and sat back to light a cigarette. His non-smoker remained empty of intrusion. The train had stopped and a voice was calling over a loud-speaker. What the . . . ? Well, it was an ordinary station announcement, he'd heard them before at this halt but what language . . . ? Always near unintelligible these broadcasts. The speaker too near the microphone, too far from diction. Today . . . a Scot, that was it! Good old British non-racialist Rail, a Scot to tell you what goes where in Sussex, they must have gone to trouble. The dialect, charming in itself he was sure, made nonsense of the nonsense—he wondered would the tweedy lady sort it out if she were not a through-to-London traveller. He glanced sideways at his manuscript and wondered, stupidly, how all that would sound read out over a public address. That was a sorting out. Did writers write as a form of do-it-yourself psychiatry? A man should be his own sorter out, no question, if he could survive it. He wondered again about the mark that might have been left on him by those adolescent queers and remembered the sorting out he had done. Helped by Basil Smart.

Basil was an actor, of some success in light comedy, who gave instruction at the Reid Foster Drama School in his resting moments. This was a problem in the running of Drama Schools, Christopher had noticed, sadly. If you wanted instructors of any worth at all you had to get them from the live theatre. The better they were the more likely they were to be earning real money, the Drama Schools paid next to nothing. Basil would arrive and, for a few weeks, would lift the hopes and spirits of the students with illuminating advice. Then he would disappear to tour with a play. When the play reached London, the students prayed —as hard as he—for a long run. This would mean they would have him in the daytime for an uninterrupted period of months, he was very popular.

As a man, out of teaching time, he was approachable and likeable. He was in his forties, had been a student here himself before the war. During which, he had been staggered to collect an M.C. In the foyer was a memorial plaque to the handful of fallen students. At the base was written LIKE STARS TO THEIR APPOINTED HEIGHT THEY CLIMB . . . AND DEATH IS A LOW MIST WHICH CANNOT BLOT THE BRIGHTNESS IT MAY VEIL . . . "Best billing they ever got" Basil had been heard to comment. "We none of us knew what we were doing in that bloody schemozzle. Medals, memorials . . ."

Basil had married a fellow student. A dolly of a girl who towered over middle heighted Basil. Rumour said somebody had christened her 'The Rake'. Red haired and sensational, Christopher thought her. Their off-student-limits meeting occurred at the annual party given so that students might meet predecessors. And Basil played a pretty good piano.

"I'm Cecily. Basil's wife".

"How do you do, I'm Christopher Tighson".

"I know. Leaving this term, aren't you?"

"Yes".

After staying only half the course again. If money can buy you learning, he thought, there's nothing like the lack of it for making you a quick study.

There had been end of term performances over the past two weeks and a week of clearing up remained. Thereafter. . . . He had been a good Lord Foppington, a passable Kit in *French Without Tears*. Hopes, plenty of hopes. But none of the students—even the paid-up two year ones—had landed more than an agent. The profession was a microcosm of the exploding world, who feeds the people?

36

"What's he playing?"

"Gershwin" said Cecily. "Basil loves Gershwin, do you like him? Or is he old hat?"

"Fits me to a T" said Christopher.

Basil, as though he had heard and saw a challenge, upped Gershwin into a very modern mood, a group of young students applauded, ran up on to the stage to dance. The cheek-to-cheek dancers there parted, in good humour, and encouraged the new girators. Cecily wandered to be near Basil, Christopher following.

"This rock and roll . . ." said Basil . . . To Cecily, he continued "Remember the parties we used to have? The eight beat I used to play? This is it all over again". To Christopher he added "We called it Boogie Woogie".

Christopher had dated a student doll for deflowering this night and was on his—not over enthusiastic—way to claim her when Basil took his arm.

"Something lined up?"

"Er . . .".

"It'll keep. It's got to. Someone I want you to meet. Cecily telephoned him, he's expecting us".

"I . . . I ought . . ."

"I understand, old lad. I'd make the same hesitation if I were your age. I'm not, worse luck. Little blond, is it?" He indicated with the merest movement of the eyes, a pretty, panting creature who had ceased to girate only a moment before and was being applauded by a small clump of admirers. Without waiting for a reply, Basil went on . . . "Bit young, even for you. Well grouped, though. I can see that you might want to get to grips with those . . . Pop over and make your excuses".

"We were . . . I was . . ."

"Of course you were. Bad luck. She'll be around next week, I suspect. Paul Bannerman won't".

"Paul . . . ?"

"Never known him to stay put. Crosses the Atlantic as often as I cross the road".

Paul Bannerman was the school's star ex-pupil. He sent

yearly apologies for not turning up at these functions, none of the students had even seen him at close quarters. He had begun as an actor—an indifferent one, reports said—but had written a very good first play during his time at the Reid Foster. It had gone to London and had been acclaimed by the critics. There had been some scandal or other, the leading girl—a student too—had flipped off to America leaving the play stranded. Susan Chase had done well in films for a spell, then had been mashed up small by the Hollywood machine. Drugs and wrist cutting. The suicide, only a year ago, had disinterred the sordid story after more than two decades of uneasy rest. Bannerman had gone to California to attend the funeral. The Press had had a field day that lasted a week and all that now remained, again, was that picture the students had wondered about in the school dining room—in character, in Paul's play. And, for the second time, a smutty legend that gave today's students a strange new status. "At the Reid-Foster, are you? Where that girl was? What's it like, do you know Paul Bannerman?" The answer to that had to be an infuriated "No" and it was back to deuce again.

Paul had drifted into acting after leaving the school, with no success at all. Later, during his war service, he had come up with a second play, a light comedy. It was the first big success of the war and he had followed it up with more of the same brittle, shallow, brilliant writing. To date, he had not one failure to his pen. He was now in a very good way indeed. George Reid and Connie Foster wished that he would visit the school, allow a little glamour to rub off. Bannerman did see to it that the school was always the first to know when a production of one of his plays was projected, so that the students might apply for the auditions. But the man himself remained a ghost.

"Of course, it's a pity. About the blonde . . ."

"I'm . . . not that keen . . ."

"You're not?" There flitted across Basil's face one of those expressions for which he was becoming known. His voice said that he was in earnest. "Nothing wrong with you, is there, old soldier?"

"No, sir".

Basil sighed. "I'm relieved to hear it. She'll keep, though. Put her on ice for a few days, it'll help no end. I've been there."

They went by taxi to Piccadilly and entered the forecourt of a building called 'Albany'.

"Not the done thing to call it '*The* Albany'" Basil said. "Can't think why. Old Byron did when he lived here". Basil alighted first, extended a hand to Cecily who didn't need it but liked the offer. Christopher tried to pay.

"Put it away, old son". As he banged shut the door of the taxi . . . "We are about to glimpse, yet again, how the other half lives".

To Christopher, as he waited for his change . . . "Or perhaps you *are* the other half, don't know much about you. Are you moneyed?"

"Good Lord no, sir".

"Pity. It's no fun earning your living, don't believe anything they say to the contrary".

"He's kidding, of course" said Cecily.

"I am not". The taxi drove away and Christopher could have sworn he heard the driver snort.

They moved through the hallway, where Basil said a word to the porter who had seen him often before, and into the country quiet of the covered 'rope walk' that led through to the Burlington exit.

"Old Paul is a bit of a recluse since . . . I suppose you read . . . ?"

"Yes".

"He's never been anything else but, really. Lives alone, never goes out. Word got round, even, that he was queer . . ."

"Really?"

Cecily chuckled.

"You hadn't heard? But perhaps you haven't come across it much, you will. The theatre is crawling with 'em".

"Basil!"

"It's the truth, old thing".

Cecily was pulling at a doorbell. Basil continued, without bitterness or any kind of emotion really. He might have been giving you the test score. "Jews and queers. If you gave them all their cards you'd close down nine tenths of the theatres in London".

"Shut up, darling".

"And the other tenth would be running at a loss. Are you a Jew, by the way?"

"Bit late to ask" said Cecily.

"Not at all" said Basil, undismayed. "I like 'em. Some of my best friends and all that. I have to confess, though, that some of my best friends are all more successful than I am".

"I'm not a Jew" said Christopher. Somehow, with Basil, it wouldn't have mattered a damn to him if he had been, Basil couldn't give offence if he tried. Everything was played lightly, skillfully. Lines were glided to leg and you'd barely notice their content in appreciating the batting. No trace of bitchery.

"Pull it again".

Cecily pulled the bell, which was old-fashioned and highly polished. They listened.

"That's better" said Basil. "It rang. It's a challenge though, old lad . . ." he went on, "If you ever do get a job it'll mean you got it in spite of what you're not more than because of what you are, if you follow me?"

"I think so, sir".

'And another thing. Now that you're no longer a student and are about to join the ranks of the normal, Christian unemployed, you can drop the 'sir'. 'Basil'."

"Basil".

"Fine. And she's Cecily, aren't you?"

The door was opened by a manservant, plainly queer and black suited, and they were taken in. "Mr. Bannerman is very sorry, sir . . . " the servant said to Basil as they walked. "He had to go across the way . . ."

"Good God, don't tell me he has an outside loo!"

"You mean to Mr. Lamont's chambers?" Cecily put in, quickly. Accustomed as he was to the comedy of Mr. Smart, The queer looked grateful.

"Yes, madam. He's been gone some time but he just

40

telephoned to say he'll be back almost at once. And will you please begin without him".

"Begin?" asked Basil.

They were in the sitting room now and Christopher noticed the Adam fireplace and eighteenth century furnishings.

"The champagne, sir". There were two bottles, both on ice.

"Oh. Oh, good. Yes, we will begin, won't we, darling? Christopher?"

The servant opened a bottle, eying Christopher the while but he was oblivious, trying to take in the room. There was so much. It was as though the tenant wished to crowd out thought with possessions. Christopher's attention was caught by an array of photographs, silver-framed, on the mantel and about the room. If Paul Bannerman was a recluse he certainly enjoyed surrounding himself with the remembrance of company. Above the fireplace was a portrait in oils of a slender girl with laughing eyes and pale blonde hair.

The manservant had left and Christopher's ex-student status gave him courage. He raised his glass to Cecily and Basil. They returned the toast and the three sipped. Christopher's gaze went back to the portrait.

"Susan Chase?" he asked Cecily.

"Yes. It's wonderful considering it was painted from photographs – and from Paul's description of her colouring . . ."

"Carrying a torch for so long you'd think your arm would drop off" said Basil. "He should have got over it, got married. To this one . . ." He had picked up a photograph and was extending it. Christopher took it and saw a serene, beautiful face that had in it a quality quite away from the startling good looks of Susan Chase. An inscription, in a wide-open hand, read simply: PAUL FROM ELIZABETH – MY LOVE.

"Was she a student?"

"Of drama, no. Horses." said Basil. "She runs a riding school in Sussex. Married a Squadron-Leader who got knocked down over Arnhem. They never found him. We see her sometimes, so does Paul. Not often enough . . ." He

41

took a gulp of champagne and asked Christopher suddenly
. . . "Do you know Sookie Lamont?"

"Neil Lamont? The manager?" Christopher called it
'La*mont.*'

"That's her. She likes the accent on the first syllable".
And Cecily said again.

"Basil!"

"Everybody calls him 'Sookie', can't think why. It must
have something to do with the nursery rhyme, you know.
'Polly put the kettle on, we'll all have tea . . . Sookie take
it off again . . .' "

"I still don't get it" said Cecily.

Basil gave her a look that, to Christopher, wasn't Basil
at all. Cecily recognised it. Basil said, "You, my love, are
an innocent". He went on, briskly, "Sookie is presenting
Paul's new play in which I am to portray a small . . ."

"It's a gorgeous part" said Cecily.

". . . but, I hope not, not ineffectual role. There's an even
smaller role that would fit you like a French letter . . .
Sorry, old girl . . ."

"Don't mind me".

"Oh but I do, indeed I do. Can't think how that slipped
out. Anyway . . ." he went on, to Christopher, "Paul wanted
to meet you and so on. I didn't mention it earlier. Never
build up the hopes too high in this game. Besides, you'll
have to get by Sookie . . ."

"Ah" said Cecily.

"Ah, indeed. Mind you, old Paul is a pretty big boy. If he
thinks you're right you're as good as in, it's only a small
role".

"Who's directing?"

Basil cleared his throat, expressively, before answering.
"He's an old bane of Paul's and mine, another Reid Foster
product. Name of St. John Pender. It's a toss-up between
him and Sookie who flies higher".

"Oh dear" said Cecily to nobody at all.

"Is he good? As a director?"

"He directed Paul's last. Nominally. It's still a smash
hit, as you know. The folk responsible are Paul who wrote
it and the two stars who, in fact, directed it. St. John's

name is on the bills though, and that makes him the most
in demand director this season, if you follow".

"Oh" said Christopher.

"Made it difficult for Paul to insist on anyone else for
the new piece. So I foresee that somebody—all of us in it,
most likely—will be spending the next few weeks pulling
St. John's second set of chestnuts out of the fire, if you'll
overlook the phrase, in order to bring home Paul's bacon
off which we too shall hope to get our year's supply of
rashers. Let's open the other bottle".

"St. John's all right" said Cecily, holding up her glass.

"Depends what you mean by 'all right', as old Joad used
to say. I can take queers if I have to but I do object to
extracting their bloody chestnuts. Sookie Lamont at least
knows his booking onions. He can tell you to a fiver just
how much you'll take in Glasgow during Fair Week, which
has its uses. Artistically he knows from sweet F.A. Sorry,
old love . . ." Cecily smiled, resigned. Basil poured and
poured and they all drank in silence. Then he took it up
again.

"Sookie has made his name by battening on the stars.
Hasn't a creative idea in his head but knows just who's
box-office and fills the bill with 'em. If he puts on a play
it's either a classic revival with three Knights and a Dame or
a new play by an author who's just had a smash hit for a
smaller manager who took a chance. The authors say 'To
hell with loyalty' and come running because Sookie has
the stars in his pocket. Why? Because he really does spend
the money and a Lamont production is a production with
with no financial holds barred. You're a name actress and
you want to be dressed by . . . what's the name . . . ?"

"Worth" Cecily put in.

"Yes, she'll do . . . Then you're dressed by . . ."

"Worth".

". . . You don't like the gowns at the Dress Parade,
Sookie'll pay for 'em, scrap 'em and you begin again
with . . ."

"Balmain" said Cecily.

"That's right. This is the third Bannerman play he's done,
authors stick to him for the same reasons as the stars . . ."

43

"Why doesn't he get the best directors? I mean, couldn't he pick brains to find out who they are?"

"You're catching on fast. He wouldn't bother. All he knows is box-office. He'll do one of two things. Either get a director who's just had three smash hits in a row—or a queer. Who may not be able to do more than riffle a script. Not to have their reputations ruined, the stars take over. And so on. If they turn out not to be capable of extracting the chestnuts and the play flops then the queer may be out. Or he may get several more tries, Sookie may blame the stars. Remember Paul's first play?" he asked Cecily. She nodded but didn't speak. Basil was on his fourth glass and she gave him the floor.

"Sookie got in a fairy film director who'd never seen a stage in his life. He had the grace to admit it. I'll never forget the first rehearsal. He made a square with his thumbs and fingers and peered at us through it. 'If this were a film' he said, 'I'd know just which lens to use . . .' He'd made quite a reputation in pictures, quite a few chestnuts get extracted in that field too. Well, he didn't stay. The actors were firm—we had a couple of topliners that would knock your eye out and Sookie beat a retreat. He paid one of them a percentage to take over the direction but the poof still had his name on the bill and still drew his! Mind you, Sookie never spends his own money, he draws the biggest management fee in the business and gets a fat rake-off but he uses the Merchant Banks. He wins when they win but when they lose, they lose alone. And the understudies, remember the understudies?"

Cecily nodded again.

"Mine was twenty years too old and it was all you could do to get him down from the flies . . . I broke my ankle in the tenth month, remember?"

Cecily said that she did.

"They had an understudy call and Paul put his foot right down. 'He can't go on' he said. 'Of course not, darling' said Sookie, 'but he's such fun to have around'. I had to play for a week in agony, with my leg in bloody plaster, while they rehearsed a replacement. And Auntie continued to attend rehearsals and be paid! With all the poor bloody actors out of work . . . Don't talk to me about Sookie".

"Nobody's said a word but you, darling".

"What? Oh. As I say, he's good at figures. What St. John Pender is good at can't be put to any use outside closed doors. But we've got him". For a moment, it seemed he had finished but there was a final flash.

"Sookie isn't even laying him!"

"Basil. Really!"

"Sorry, old love. But he isn't. St. John is set up very nicely somewhere else. But . . ." He waved his empty glass to say that he was at a loss. But he wasn't. "There's this freemasonry . . . You can't lick it, he's got the stars tied up, he's got all the lush theatres . . . In this case, he's got Paul . . . Diplomacy, all is diplomacy. But it gets on your bloody wick, where's old Paul?"

As though in further apology and in consolation, the man-servant brought in more champagne, placed it at the ready and went out, closing a silent door. It was a false exit because the telephone rang and, after answering it elsewhere, he returned to ask Basil to pick up the sitting-room extension.

"Paul? Not at all, we're well into the second bottle . . ."

"We've finished it" Cecily said.

"We've finished it . . . Oh . . . Not at all old lad. Of course I'll explain. I'll call you in the morning. No, I won't, you call me" Christopher heard what he took to be a healthy laugh at the other end and the conversation was concluded.

"He's going to be tied up for a late session" Basil explained. To Cecily he said "Let's take the boy to the Caprice. We can watch the lions feed while we eat, it's always good for a laugh".

"Er . . . this *is* a non-smoker?"

Christopher looked up to see a figure in an expensive but over cut fawn suit hovering in the doorway.

"Of course. I'm so sorry . . ." He looked about him, damn British Rail, no ash-tray . . . He stood up to open the slide window and broke a nail . . .

"Please, my dear boy. I'd like to smoke too, it's quite all right".

He managed a controlled sit, leaned back to examine his finger nail, then to read. The newcomer sat directly opposite, choosing this seat from five available—three of which would have given polite distance. Christopher knew that a scrutiny had begun. With one, brief upward glance he caught enough of the picture to look down again at once. He saw a neat man of fifty something. A pink, smooth face. The hair dark but with that golden glow about the hairline roots that proclaims the dye bottle. And makes the user look ten years older, perhaps he was forty something? The stiff white collar just a touch too tight above the lilac shirt, squeezing up the flesh of the neck, the mauve tie not everybody's cup of neckwear, but expensive, very. Fawn suit, atop the head a fawn bowler—the brim over curled to a point of caricature. So expensive, so extreme, so over careful the whole effect—patterned pocket handkerchief, down to the fawn silk socks and the hand cut, weathered tan shoes—so much an outward expression of the inward man or whatever that one would not laugh. In fact, he carried it off. If not with triumph, with a defiant assurance.

No single feature, natural or tailored, shouted homo like

the eyes. Bright, needle sharp, they danced at you. On points. Basil Smart had taught him immediate homo recognition.

"Christopher?"

"Basil?"

"Yes, I'm calling about Paul Bannerman, he telephoned this morning. Can you be in Lamont's office at three o'clock, they want to look you over".

"Fine. I can't tell you how grateful . . ."

"Never mind that. Be there. And I should stuff a cork well in, call me tonight?"

Christopher entered a famous London theatre, one of the lush, Lamont controlled group and was shown into a small lift that led up to the offices. Once the gate was closed, you worked it by hand and—he supposed—thanked God you were alone. The addition of one other passenger would mean a physical nearness that could be tricky in the extreme and you could say that again. He was greeted at the top by, presumably, a secretary? No, she was too old for that, a casting director? Thin, efficient looking, in glasses. And hideously ugly. Basil was to opine to him later "Beware of a woman who is popular with queers. She will be mannish, grotesque or a tramp . . . or have some quality, however subtle, that might be considered to let down her sex. She may merely be ugly . . ."

"Christopher Tighson?"

"Yes".

"How do you do, my name is Cowles. I'm Mr. Lamont's general manager. He and Mr. Pender are in the main office with Mr. Bannerman. They're waiting for you".

"I'm . . . not late?"

"No, indeed not. This way . . ."

He was taken along a deeply carpeted passage and Miss Cowles opened a door at the end.

"Mr. Tighson" she announced and he passed her into the room. The door closed behind him, Miss Cowles had gone.

47

The room had a window at the far end that overlooked roof tops. Its carpet was even deeper than the one in the passage, the furniture over stuffed, over polished, the curtaining heavy—like a plushy eagle's nest, he thought. The eagle himself sat behind a huge desk, in the window alcove. He had his back to the light and toyed with some piece of desk accoutrement, the flat top had all of these, Christopher had seen them laid out in Asprey's windows and wondered who ever used them. A willowy figure posed at his side, half in shadow. Christopher was being greeted.

"Christopher Tighson. I'm Paul Bannerman, how do you do".

He took the extended hand, the grip was firm but not the sort of grip that tried to prove anything. Bannerman should have been taller, he felt, as tall as he. But there was a slight stoop to bring down the broad shoulders. A frank face, fair hair, grey eyes. They didn't dance.

"How do you do, sir".

Paul introduced him to Neil Lamont who sprang from his chair and came tripping round to the front of the desk to offer a well manicured hand. Christopher took it, noted that it was soft, built for toying. The hand kneaded his a little and Christopher said—with only the merest of emphases on the designation . . .

"Mr. Lamont". He remembered to put the accent where the manager liked it to be.

"I'm St. John Pender" came, in a soft—strangely deep—voice, from the window. They exchanged a smile. Christopher was conscious that Sookie was very near to him.

"Well, my boy . . ." he began, "There's a part we'd like you to play in Mr. Bannerman's new comedy . . ." A small emphasis in return? Christopher was certain that Neil Lamont would never miss a trick. ". . . If you're not otherwise engaged?"

"No" said Christopher. His legs had gone weak.

"Sit down, sit down" Lamont said, waving a hand towards an expensive but very uncomfortable looking Regency piece. Gold flashed from the wrist that belonged to the hand. Christopher sat—on something and rose immediately.

"It's my new hat" said Lamont, his eyes dancing a Flamenco.

"I say . . . I'm most terribly sorry . . ." Christopher picked up a crumpled felt hat, the squashy kind that isn't meant to be squashed. He looked in Paul's direction but Paul had turned his back and was leaning on the mantel, his hand covering his mouth.

"Toss it aside, just toss it aside". Lamont retreated to behind the desk, exchanging a look with Pender. "St. John is directing, of course" he was saying. "Do you think he'd be right, St. John?"

Christopher doubted that Pender would disagree with Lamont in anything. He would be praying both for success and continued patronage. Had Lamont—or Bannerman, given him a lead?

"Absolutely" Pender said.

"Paul?"

"I agree" said Paul.

"Wouldn't you like me to read?"

A peal of high pitched laughter came from Neil Lamont who leaned back in his Hepplewhite elbow chair, stroking the arms. "Now, that's what I like, keenness" he said. "Do you want the boy to read, St. John?"

"No" Pender ventured with a little shrug.

"Paul?"

Paul clipped the wings of the situation. "Basil Smart's recommendation is good enough for me" he said. Warmly, to Christopher . . . "He spoke very highly indeed". Lamont had pressed an intercom and Miss Cowles' voice came through.

"Would you give Mr. Tighson a script and a list of the dates. Have you an agent?" he asked Christopher.

"No, sir".

"He doesn't employ an agent, arrange terms with him . . ." To Christopher . . . "I *hate* talking money, Miss Cowles will be very generous . . . Miss Cowles, will you arrange an appointment with the tailor and see that Jeremy goes with him, I want no mistakes. Mr. Tighson must look divine . . ." To Christopher . . . "Don't you want to look

49

divine . . . it's South of Francey, lovely casuals, you know
. . ." To Paul . . . "You think, shorts . . . ?"

"Trousers would be better".

"Trousers, Miss Cowles. But tight as a drum, he must
be poured into them". He clicked the intercom and sat
back, stroking the arms again. "There" he said. And the
eyes pierced Christopher all over, like an Iron Maiden.

"Basil?"

"Christopher?"

"Yes. I got the part".

"Hurray. Sex rear its ugly nob?"

"Er . . . not so's you wouldn't notice it".

Basil chuckled at the other end of the line. "You'll be all
right. What do you think of the play?"

Christopher had read it in Lyons over tea and a cherry
bakewell. He thought it brilliant and said so.

"Like the part?"

"It's only one scene but what a scene! I hope I can do
it".

"Do it, of course you can do it! There are at least six
laughs. Come round tomorrow and I'll show you you can
make it a dozen. Cecily will cook lunch for us, all right?"

"All right. Thank you, sir".

" 'Basil' ".

"Basil".

Rearsals for *Lady in the Sun* were an eye opener to
Christopher. At the Reid Foster—especially with Basil
Smart—they had been well run. But fallibility gave them
warmth. You tried and failed and you were shown where
you failed. In Lamont productions failure went unremarked.
It was assumed you wouldn't fail but if you did—as long
as you didn't make the set collapse—there were a dozen
hushers-up. Who expected that, in return, you would keep
mum about their failures. Failure became a currency. A
shiny, gold looking medallion that, with sleight of theatrical

hand, was palmed, revealed again, passed. It was not the done thing to bring failure out into the open.

"The curtains are horrid".

"It's the material, it just won't make up. I told Jeremy when it was chosen".

"Jeremy!"—in not more than a smack bottom tone.

"Don't blame Jeremy . . ." (He might blame me?) . . . "He was told it had been dyed with a special new substance. If you ask me, they dipped it in Lucozade . . ." Laughter filled the stalls and an instruction was given that the curtains be scrapped.

"Order new ones".

"They'll *never* be ready!" tearfully, from the designer who was Jeremy's side-kick, Jeremy was really 'Clothes'.

"What is it, Thursday? Let them work round the clock".

"It'll cost".

A silence. It answered the side-kick who scuttled away, his speed an apology for bringing up the taboo subject.

Christopher was relieved to have seen little of Sookie. He appeared only when every possible failure had had the icing caked over it. He would have liked to see more of Paul but, if he was there, his presence was unfelt by actors or director. Sometimes a figure could be glimpsed at the back of the circle . . .

"Are you still with us, Christopher?" Pender had said at last. He resolved not to look again.

The male star, as forecast, took over the direction but not as a paid percentage earner, Pender was having none of that. St. John had, it seemed, evolved a technique of asking advice as though he were inviting the actor to have his head. The advice given, he would say, "I *knew* that was how you would feel it. And you know what? That's just how I want it, let's run it again".

He deceived nobody. But then, nobody deceived anybody, it appeared to Christopher. All were working in mask behaviour and the important thing was never—on or off the play set—to let your mask slip. Keep passing the currency.

The two female stars were at loggerheads. One—the more talented—thought the male star was right in his directorial take-over bids. The other whined unwise exception. So that the male star's subtler suggestions—which St. John Pender would have been happy to incorporate—were brought dangerously near to blow-up.

"Who *is* directing this play?" she asked, once. This broke the unbreakable Lamont rule. If you were going to have a success at all and you were given a director like St. John Pender—"His first is still running, darling!", the least you could do was to extract chestnuts quietly. You just didn't make a song and dance. Wisely, the male star bowed to St. John who, covered in ineptitude, was forced to make the wrong decision which damaged an exit of the objecting female star. Who, from then on, was sweetness and tractability.

Basil, as a feature player, might have stayed in hotels for the tour. But he preferred digs. "The worst digs are better than most four star hotels" he said. "I stay in the best". And he gave his list to Christopher.

"But you and Cecily will want to be alone . . ."

"Don't be a twot, old man. Opening date—Manchester, as I live and choke—we'll brave the Midland, show the flag. After that, digs. Now, they nearly always have a double room and bath, Cecily and I will bag that. And at least one single which you can have. You may have to hop into the bath with the landlady but they're very sweet. Mine are. A fast declining race, pure gold the ones I know. Some of them have daughters who, by now, are beginning to burst out of their twin sets. Don't put 'em in the family way, of course. And write now. I'd rather share digs with you than that faggot of an A.S.M. who loses his place in the book".

Christopher looked out at the over green countryside. Lush with day after day rain it was, all Nature had bolted like a lettuce. The foliage was one great, luxuriant beard covering the face of the earth. Today was a day of sunlight and the sun searched the earth, mocking it for the lack of self discipline, tugging the beard on the face. Why this imbalance in nature? If it rains too hard, too constantly, is there no automatic cut-out? Must that which is naturally within be drawn to full exposure and stand ashamed when the light hits? His eyes, looking through the compartment window, drew back their focus, saw the window itself and the image there.

"Would you care for one of mine?"

Christopher became aware that he was reaching for another cigarette. "Thank you, I . . . Thank you". He accepted the fat offered cigarette, not wanting it, not wanting to smoke. Before he could reach for his lighter there was a flash of gold and a trim flame made an obedient, one click appearance.

"Forgive me . . ." he said, forestalling the conversation that had been so prologued, "I must do this . . . reading . . ."

"But of course".

Christopher drew in smoke that was tinged with scent, and went on with his study.

The fellow passenger was not smoking. For a long moment he continued to stare at Christopher. Then he took up a copy of The Times and opened it. At an angle that would give him permission to look over it at Christopher whenever he felt the urge to fondle with his gaze.

Lady in the Sun had opened a two-week season at the Manchester Opera House, with expected acclaim. You got a national Press coverage, but from northern critics. The southern ones, writing on the southern editions of the same newspapers, weeks later, would not—of necessity— support their northern colleagues. And yet . . . one waited for the northern notices. If they were bad you could say that it augured well for a London critical reversal. If they were good, you were pleased but cagey. "Let's not count our chickens". But you were pleased, you wouldn't be human if you weren't. The one certain thing being that tour notices didn't make a damn of difference. In the case of a Lamont play, that was. If you had an untried author, a smaller management—both of which factors would mean indifferently drawing leads, a bad or good Press could bring you a bigger or smaller audience. Perhaps. The power or the impotence of the Press.

After the opening—in a theatre the size of Clapham Junction and with as little of the necessary atmosphere, it seemed to Christopher, Basil and Cecily took him back to the Midland for supper. They sat at a corner table. Lamont, Pender and Paul Bannerman at a table some distance away. Christopher cast a nervous side glance in its direction.

"Sookie come round to see you?"

"Yes".

"What did he say?"

"Er . . ."

"Go on" said Cecily. "You're among friends".

"He said I was entrancing".

Basil choked on his wine and Cecily went a delightful shade of smiling pink. Christopher was beginning to like her a lot.

"Splendid!" said Basil. "What did you say back?"

"Er . . . I said thank you, sir".

"Good. Non-commital. They're having a post mortem over there".

Paul had risen from his table and was coming towards them.

"Want to know something?" said Basil, watching the approach. "I'm not going to get any sleep until the papers. Paul".

"Basil, you old . . ." Paul looked with enormous affection at Cecily and they clasped hands. Then he mimed a punch at Basil's chin. "You were bloody marvellous" he said.

"Thanks".

"So were you, lad", to Christopher. "Sit down, we're attracting attention".

Christopher sat. And Paul pulled a chair from a nearby, empty table and sat with them. "I think Sookie's pleased . . ." he began.

"He bloody well should be. So should St. John, 'grateful' is the word. To all of us, even you".

"Shut up. Get-together upstairs? Sookie's suite in about twenty minutes? Sorry, Cecily".

"It's routine" said Basil. "I don't mind Sookie picking my brains. It's the only reason he employs me . . ."

"Balls" said Cecily, to Christopher's surprise. Nobody else raised half an eyebrow.

"The lady's right" Paul said. "In any case it's I who want to pick your brains".

"That's different. It's not the only reason you write a part for me. But don't tell me Sookie will ever know a performance from the hole in his . . ."

"Basil" said Cecily.

"You said 'balls', why can't I say 'arse'?"

"Not in front of the L.A.D." Paul said.

Basil said to Christopher, "Chris, why don't you look in in the morning? Not too early, why not noon?"

"Why not for lunch?" asked Cecily.

"I've just had supper".

"So, who's counting? When you get your play put on I shall expect the lead. I might settle for the father by then. No offence, old sausage".

"Has Christopher written a play?" Paul asked.

Basil said, "Oh, shit. Was it confidential?"

"Of course not" said Christopher. "And I haven't. I mean, I have but I haven't quite. If you follow".

"No" said Paul and Basil in unison. If you didn't know it, this one comedy team reaction would tell you these friends were near.

"I've written. But I haven't finished".

"Ah" said Paul. "I know the feeling. I have one myself, on the stocks, but the skin is not yet mounted on the bones. To my satisfaction. Hey, young Chris . . . Come to sup tomorrow night? Here? With me?"

Christopher's apparent hesitation was due to cardiac near failure. As a young juvenile actor, you were not asked out by a lion playwright. Unless he was after your bum—as Basil had put it many a time. And he knew, or hoped he knew, that Paul wasn't.

Basil was saying, "Never say 'no' to an offer that includes food". He added the now familiar red light phrase—or nearly did . . . "Unless it's an offer that includes . . .'

"Basil" said Cecily.

"Sorry, old lady. But you gather my drift?"

"Yes" said Christopher. To Paul he said "I'd like it very much, sir".

"Don't 'sir' me for Christ's sake. 'Paul' ".

"Paul".

"I'll pick you up after what is laughingly called 'the play'. And before anybody says a word about that, don't". He had risen from the table, his expression sad and strangely firm. Forbidding argument. "Cecily. My 'sorries'. Basil, my gratitude. Both . . . my love. See you tomorrow, youngster and don't slam the door on your exit, you might get a round".

A moment of silence followed his leaving them. Then Basil said "That's two more meals you've got yourself".

The notices were hysterically in favour of 'the slickest comedy writing of our times'. 'The wit that continues to come from the Paul Bannerman . . . conveyor belt . . . was that praise? One critic counted the laughs, a hundred and eighty-seven. How the hell could you watch a play and listen *and* count the laughs? Basil came in for high praise and Christopher's name was mentioned in every paper. Only one comment, though . . . '. . . promising newcomer who, with his looks, is certain to be snapped up into films'. Was *that* praise?

Christopher remembered not to slam the door but closed it too gently for wood and canvas. After his exit, it swung open and had to be closed again by Basil who was to follow with a comedy scene and was too old a hand to play it in competition with an open door. The faggot A.S.M. fluttered up to Christopher in the wings.

"You forgot to close the door" he hissed, a little triumphantly.

"I didn't forget".

"You didn't close it".

"Yes" said Christopher and turned to go.

"Don't forget to apologise to Mr. Smart".

A traditionalist faggot, full marks. He wouldn't have forgotten, it had been drummed into him in his training. By Basil Smart.

He trekked across the vast stage, stepping on the coconut matting that softened the noise. Then through the door on the O.P. side to climb the six flights of stairs that led to the top floor where were to be found the understudies' room, the wardrobe and one or two dressing rooms for the small part players. He was the only such player in *Lady in the Sun*, Bannerman packed his casts pretty neatly, this play had only seven characters. Five were leading or feature. Even the butler was the best part old Alec Rhodes had ever had, thirty four laughs, not including the chuckles. The juvenile girl had been on the stage for three years and had a part three times as long as Christopher's but not as rewarding. He had a ten minute cameo and in the last act, a dream of a situation for a beginner. The juvenile girl dressed on the floor below and had beautiful legs and boobs —she had to strip off in the play which was set in St. Tropez. Christopher had hopes of stripping her off himself before the tour was much older. She was sitting in his room.

"Jacqueline".

"Thought I'd pay a visit. Do you mind?"

"Welcome to the top floor. You went over big tonight".

"It's because I nearly fell out of my bikini. You were getting lots of laughs, I heard you on the Tannoy. What d'you think of the notices?"

"Super. I hope we get a year".

"So do I. I've been in two flops in a row—one of them for Sookie".

"He doesn't have many. How are your digs?"

"Awful. How are yours?'

"Marvellous. Basil gave me them, a little way out of the town but marvellous".

"I get spam every night".

"Mine gives me a bloody great roast. All I can do to get through it. Sorry".

She was a pretty little thing and her face had fallen. "Why don't you move?" he asked.

"Move where to?"

"Mrs. Tuffnell's got other rooms. I'm the only one staying".

"Chris! That'd be super, would you mind?"

"Mind? It'd be company. Especially on the bus ride home. Why don't you . . . ?" He hesitated. She carried his thought on for him . . .

"Could I come back with you? Tonight? Have a look see and fix it up?"

"Er . . . I have to go out tonight".

"You have a date in Manchester?"

"With Paul".

'Bannerman? Whoops! Sorry".

"What do you mean, 'sorry'?"

"Isn't he . . . I hope you're not . . . It's none of my business anyway . . ."

"Isn't he what?"

"Well, you know . . . Queer".

"Is he buggery!"

They both laughed at his choice of a word. "Sorry, I shouldn't have said 'buggery' ".

They laughed again. He went on . . . "Come round first thing tomorrow. I'll write down the address. Masses of hot water and Mrs. Tuffnell's a peach. And you can help me out with the roasts".

Her face lit up and she gave him a little, warm kiss— only just not on the lips. He hadn't had a girl for nearly two months, last time Basil had bitched it up, tonight it was Paul. Sod the old generation, he thought. Over rehearsals, fear and worry had put sex out of mind but one warm kiss and he was half way up the dressing room wall.

"That was nice . . ." he began.

The Tannoy on the wall said "All down for the final curtain!" Christopher knew fully, for the first time, the exquisite value of delay.

CHAPTER

8

The old generation took over the late evening and proved, again, to Christopher that it could attract irresistibly. Contempt for it, by the new, was high fashion but Christopher didn't like the fit of the garment. He had affection—and, he thought, respect—for the Templars. So they bitched up the peace after the first war, who was going to do better between now and the next? The Templars trusted the wrong politicians, their crime was faith. Who are the right politicians? And what now, the era of no faith? Christopher had known just enough of war not to be mere pacifist. The courage of the conscientious objector would get no medals from him. If you turned the cheek and let the bastards walk in and take over this was biblical strength, maybe. But it didn't do a thing for your balls.

As Paul and he sat at supper, Christopher glanced about him.

"Looking for Sookie?"

"I was, yes".

"He took off by plane for London. He has three new productions coming up—no time to sit in Manchester and hold our hands. Thank God?"

Paul smiled meaningly across the table. Damned good looking he is, thought Christopher. Lucky he has this talent and Sookie needs him without strings. Good playwrights were few, actors many. Paul seemed to read something of this.

"Tell me about your play. If you want to, of course. I promise not to pinch the idea".

"It's . . . I don't know, I've barely finished the first draft . . . It's about a drama school . . ."

"A subject fresh in mind, that's good. In three acts?"

"Yes".

"Exposition in the first but plenty of movement too? Problems reaching a peak in the second? And a whacking great surprise in the third—about ten minutes before the final curtain? Those ten minutes are the hardest, go on".

Suddenly, Christopher felt that he hadn't written a play at all. "I never thought of it like that".

"You just took up a pen and began to write, did you? Your dialogue good?"

"Yes" said Christopher, encouraged. "Yes, I think it is good".

"It's the biggest trap in the world. Let's go upstairs and I'll show you what I mean. Coffee?"

"I'd like some, yes".

"Coffee in my suite" Paul said to the waiter and they went up.

A hotel suite can be impersonal. Paul's sitting-room had the look of an impersonal florist's. Flowers stood on every available piece of furniture and there are always too many of these. On the mantel, even, where the coal fire was causing them to wilt. Two framed photographs gave personality. One of Susan Chase. The other of the girl who ran the riding school—Elizabeth?

"Here's my first go at *Lady in the Sun,* Paul was saying.

60

He had produced a hard-cover exercise book. The waiter brought coffee in and set it on the one undecorated table, before the sofa.

"Care for a liqueur, sir?" he asked Paul.

"Christopher?"

"Not for me".

Paul dismissed the waiter and they sat side by side. "If you're worrying about the flowers they're mostly from Sookie. I expect you got some?"

"I got something in a pot".

"That's standard. In three weeks time we play Oxford. Sookie has a country home nearby and you'll be asked to spend the week-end. On the way to Brighton".

"Oh?"

"I assume you can take care of yourself?"

"I think so".

"Good. Take care of that pot plant too, he'll ask you how it's going. It'll break his heart if you tell him you threw it in the ash can".

"I didn't".

"Good. Now. *Lady in the Sun* . . ."

He opened the exercise book and edged nearer to Christopher who hoped to hell Jacqueline wasn't right. He didn't think she was. Paul pointed to the first page.

"Characters. With names, I like to take hold of the names and hope they'll take hold of me in some way. At a later stage, of course. Am I talking cock?"

"No, sir".

" 'Paul' ".

"Paul".

"Having given them names. I give them numbers—A to whatever. G, in this this case . . . Now . . ." He turned the page. "Setting" he said. "I go into this at quite some length, again hoping it will talk something back".

Another page turned. "Act One, Scene One. Take a look". Christopher took a look and thought he was back to Euclid. He read:

Scene (two minute maximum) between A and F. Establish following:—

(i) Locale (also villa, hotel?)

61

(ii) Time of year.

(iii) Time of day.

These three points were bracketed and had the words '4—8 speeches' written beside them. The page continued:

(iv) Relationships.

(v) Reasons for presence here—expected length of stay.

G enters, by appointment (this may or may not be but references in Acts Two and Three will have bearing). Presence obviously objected to by F who dismisses A (on pretext or summarily?) and proceeds to question G. Scene follows, of not more than three minutes duration, in which . . .

Christopher accepted Paul's invitation to drink a little of the brandy he travelled. And he drank his coffee in one.

"Look thorough?" Paul asked, as he rose to do the pouring.

"Yes".

"It isn't, of course, every playwright's way of working but it's mine. And it pays off. You're not left with surplus stuff, everything your people do or say is relevant and the action moves on to its correct peaks at selected moments".

"I see".

"Of course, this is the second working book, the first is illegible. Scrawling about the story line, scoring out, insert marks . . . By the time I get to this second book, I know where I'm going in vague terms—not so vague, pretty exact . . . This is the building of the guts . . ." Paul had drunk his brandy and was replenishing. His mind seemed to be a mile away.

"More?" he asked—with an apparent rudeness that Christopher knew to be merely a bump back to earth. He hadn't begun on his first.

"No, thank you".

"All this is to tell you that I don't—until the very last— begin on dialogue. I'm good, too, at writing dialogue . . ." Christopher gave a gasp to indicate that this was putting it small. Paul caught the reaction and brushed it aside with impatience. "A lot of playwrights are. This is easy to be good at. And, therefore, the last brilliance to be indulged. When you know exactly where you're going in general, with whom and for how long and leading up to what in particular, then . . . you may pen a line of dialogue and not before. That's if you're me".

He was looking away from Christopher and seemed to be addressing a gathering . . . "For the most part", he concluded, "you may thank God you're not". He continued to look away.

There was a pause, during which Christopher told himself he had been present at a rare instruction. It was Paul's way of working but he knew that it must be, at least, the kind of discipline one had to make oneself subject to. Where did the inspiration come in, where the heart? In the original story line, the illegible Book One? Was it, in fact, possible —as he had done—to launch straight into dialogue, be carried along by a subconscious directive and with the story line loosely considered, left open and subject to adjustment that may be dictated by the dialogue itself?

"I will have another, if I may?"

Paul poured—for both of them—and Christopher saw that the instruction had taken quite a lot out of him. He was tired, pale . . . drinking too freely? And the sadness never left his eyes. "Tell me more about yours. What have you called it?"

"I . . . just have a working title . . . *The Reprobate* . . ."

"Not bad. Must have something the moron public can pronounce, though. Always picture them on the telephone to Keith Prowse . . . 'I'd like two seats for . . .'. If they get nervous, they may switch to *Charlie's Aunt*".

"It's a working title. It won't do".

"Coward picked *Present Laughter* from Shakespeare, *Blithe Spirit* from Shelley . . . *This Happy Breed*, Shakespeare again. He's pretty good as a source for titles, the Bard . . ."

"I did think of *Infants of the Spring* . . .'

Paul was a very long moment in replying . . . "Yes. Laertes. Too whimsy for a play, not bad for a novel. May I read it?"

"Read it? Would you?"

"If you'd like me to".

"I'd be very flattered".

"Balls. Drop it round to me in the morning and I'll read

it before I go back to London. I shall get the evening plane. You want a frank opinion?"

"Of course".

" 'Of course' is meaningless, nobody wants a frank opinion, only praise. That's what I like, anyway. But you'll get a frank opinion".

They drank a little, talked a great deal, Paul drank again —alone. Then Christopher ventured a question. "Your first play, Paul . . . The one you wrote at the Reid Foster . . ."

Another long moment. Christopher was about to continue when Paul answered "*Galatea*, yes?"

"Did you use the same technique?"

He might have hit Paul in the pit of the stomach. Paul drained his glass before answering, "You're a penetrating young bastard . . ."

"I'm sorry . . ."

"Don't be, there's no need. No. I wrote *Galatea* just as I am sure you wrote *The Reprobate*, straight out of my innocent bowels. The thing to remember about bowels is that they don't remain innocent. You can only spill them once, after that you have to pick 'em up and sort 'em out and put 'em back. With luck, one day . . . they may be ready to spill again but, by Christ, it takes it out of you . . ."

He lapsed into silence and Christopher looked at his watch.

"Missed the last bus? Basil said he'd given you his digs, I stayed there once".

"You did?"

"During my early, unillustrious acting period". He picked up the telephone.

"I'll stand you a taxi".

"Don't, please! I can . . ."

"You won't get paid till Friday, I've been paid. Shut up". He ordered the taxi, arranging payment with the porter, and repeated his request to have Christopher's script in the morning.

"One for the lift?"

"No, really. It's been a super evening, Paul. Thank you".

"Please. How old are you?"

They were on their way to the door and Christopher turned to answer. "I'll be twenty two next week".

"Twenty two". Then there occurred a moment of great worry for Christopher. Paul took his face in both his hands and looked searchingly at him. Oh Jesus, no, Christopher thought. With his left hand still on Christopher's cheek, Paul caressed his head with the right, smoothing the hair back. Then he ruffled it a little, mimed a punch at his chin and said, "Goodnight, infant".

Christopher continued in speculation throughout the taxi ride to his digs. Mrs. Tuffnell was still up.

"Nice hot cup of soup?" she asked.

"No thank you, Mrs. Tuffnell. You didn't wait up for me?"

"No, love" she lied. "I had things to do. Cup of tea?"

"Nothing, thank you". As she turned to go . . . "Mrs. Tuffnell . . ."

"Ay?"

"You have a visitors' book?"

"Ay. You'll be signing it at the end of the week, I hope".

"Of course. Could I see it? Now?"

"It's in parlour. Right hand drawer of sideboard".

Christopher thumbed back through the pages to 1937 and saw Paul's neat signature. In the 'Remarks' column he had written: 'Wonderful time, Mrs. T. Only one problem. Where do we go from here . . . ?'

E

9

"Buffet car forward" the voice said.

Christopher surfaced from contemplation and his eyes met the pair across from him.

"Nice of them to tell us" said the fawn creature who owned the eyes. "It was nicer still when they brought the coffee to you in your seat. Will you join me?" he was standing now and Christopher noticed again the over waisting of the jacket.

"Thank you no, I must get on with this".

"Can I bring you something back?"

Christopher wanted to say "Yes, coffee and biscuits, not too much milk and no sugar" but he dreaded involvement.

"It's kind of you. But, no".

A whiff of scent was carried to him as the door slid open, and the fawn man was gone. Christopher looked across at the bowler hat and umbrella, placed neatly in the rack. If he ever put an umbrella in the rack it was goodbye to the umbrella because he never could become involved with railway compartments either. He travelled self contained, putting such articles as he carried on the seat beside him. That was the limit to his allowed attachment to a moving conveyance. Some people even used the guard's van . . . "Jackie's boobs," he thought suddenly. And went back to contemplation.

Jackie came at nine thirty and Christopher was still sound asleep.

"There's a young lady" said Mrs. Tuffnell. "I showed her in the parlour, she says you said I might have a room . . ."

"What? Oh, good morning, Mrs. Tuffnell. What?"

"A young lady. She . . ."

"Oh Lord, I forgot, yes. Have you a room, Mrs. T.?"

"I haven't been called that for twenty years".

"I'm sorry . . ."

"I like it. But nobody's called me that . . ."

"Have you? A room? She's from the theatre, she's very nice. And not very happy where she is".

"She can have the one next to yours" said Mrs. Tuffnell, with the straightest face he'd seen.

"Oh. Ah. She'll be glad. Where is she?"

"I said. In the parlour. What do you want for breakfast, the usual?"

"Could you make it for two, Mrs. T.? I have a feeling she won't have had the usual".

Christopher threw on a robe and went down the stairs in two leaps.

"Jacqueline! Jack, Jackie—which?"

"Jack. 'Morning".

"All fixed up, Jackie. Had breakfast?"

"Yes".

"Not the usual, you haven't. Off with your coat and sit down. How's that for a fire?" he said proudly.

"Wonderful. My place is a morgue".

"No it isn't, this is your place from now on. I'll go round with you later to collect your things. Rehearsal call is . . . eleven thirty?"

"Yes".

"Time for everything. I shall hop into a bath . . . Do you want one?"

"Not now. I had a cold bath last night".

"Then, after rehearsal you come straight back here and get into a hot one. I might even scrub your back".

"What about Mrs. Tuffnell?"

"I don't mind scrubbing hers too. She's marvellous.

67

Right now, she's preparing the biggest breakfast you ever saw. Give me eight minutes".

In ten, he was back, shaved and shining. And they sat down to mounds of bacon and two eggs each—"More on the hob"—and Jackie announced that she had thawed out.

"You don't know what it is in this weather, plastering your body with brown and dancing round in a bikini. I have the utmost difficulty in conveying the sunshine of St. Tropez".

"I never thought of it".

"Of course you didn't. And when you get back at night, you have to scrape it all off. My skin is like a nut-meg grater. All over".

"Oh," said Christopher, who didn't quite believe it. "No natural oils?"

"There were once. I say . . . Could I have another egg?" At that moment, Mrs. Tuffnell brought in a dish with a cover. She lifted it and, without a word, slid an egg on to each of their plates.

"More bacon?" she asked.

"Mrs. T. . . ." said Christopher, "We shall be back for lunch. Latish, about one-thirty . . . And, if we are not to disappoint you by not eating our second helping . . . Unless, of course . . ?" Jackie shook her head. "No bacon" he concluded.

Mrs. Tuffnell's chubby face collapsed into a confusion of wrinkles and dimples and she went out, very happy.

"See what I mean, Jackie?"

" 'Jack'."

"It might seem I'm tagging around with a fella".

"Are you worried?"

"No".

"All right. Make it 'Jackie' if you'd rather. Make Christopher happy" she said.

They collected her things from Ackers Street and she paid her dues. (A full week it had to be, the landlady was not one of the declining race, she was on the way in.) And took a bus that dropped them near the Midland Hotel. Christopher left his literary package at the reception desk and they walked down to the Opera House.

The rehearsal call was for changes in pace, the excision of hold up 'business'—put in by St. John Pender and proven to be signally unfunny.

"How was last night?" Basil asked during a lull.

"Fine. Paul is going to read my play".

"Delighted to hear it. I'd have made the offer myself but in the first place I can't read and even if I could I couldn't read a play. Actors can't. Is he taking it with him to London?"

"Said he'd read it before he goes".

"My word, you did make an impression. How's Mother Tuffnell?"

"She's fine. I'm putting on pounds. Jacqueline has just moved in . . ." He wondered why he had added that and whether he should have.

"Ah" said Basil. "By the way, did you ever get around to making the little blonde? The one whose evening I spoiled?"

"No".

"Sorry about that. I should think Jackie'll be more fun. Don't worry about Mrs. T., she was brought up to such things by early boarders. And the house is as solid as a rock".

They had hot pot for lunch, followed by treacle pudding. Jackie had spent half an hour in a steaming bath and sat in a white towelling robe, her dyed blond hair falling in tousled chaos over her shoulders. She had been made to dye it for the play—from a natural dark chestnut—and had hated the change.

"It's beginning to fall out" she said now to Christopher.

"Your hair? Good Lord, why?"

"It's this bloody peroxide. They did warn me in London. My hair doesn't take it unless they do it three or four times, it's agony". Why the hell sexy ladies in plays always have to be blondes I wouldn't know. It's you men who do it. You'd never tell a dirty story about a man in bed and

69

in walks a beautiful brunette, would you? It's always a blonde. Why?"

"I wouldn't know either. I thought it was very pretty at rehearsal".

"It was Sookie. Paul said it was fine as it was but Sookie insisted. I think he knew it would hurt. He foots the bills, at least. When it all falls out he can pay for a wig".

"It looks all right to me".

"You don't have to comb it. It comes out in lumps. And it doesn't look all right, I look like a man in drag".

"Not from where I'm sitting. What about a picture this afternoon?"

"I'd love it but I have an appointment at the hairdresser".

"You don't half go through it for your art".

"And I have to go searching for body make-up. I've tried just about every one there is, they all flay the skin off you. Never be a woman".

"I shall do my best to avoid a change. What time will I see you?"

"God knows. I'll probably go straight to the theatre. Thanks for being so sweet, Chris. It's going to be lovely here . . ."

She gazed gratefully at the fire, too, stretching, her arms wide. Her robe opened at the bosom as she stretched and settled loosely, revealingly, as her arms came down. She smiled at Christopher . . . "I must get dressed".

She gave him another warm little kiss and was gone.

Christopher got in early to the theatre and found a large envelope waiting for him. He went up the stairs four at a time, threw open his door and flopped, panting, into a chair. He's read it. And has delivered it in person—or had it sent round! He waited for several minutes before opening the envelope. Telling himself that, whatever the verdict, he, young Chris, was a happy, bloody lucky man. His name in Paul's handwriting. He cut the top of the envelope with scissors, not wanting to damage it, and took out his script. Inside the cover was a letter—again, in Paul's hand . . .

'Dear Chris,

I read it at once, knowing what a hell it is to be kept waiting. It is, as I feared, a disorganised group of ideas and the dramatic impact just isn't there. The dialogue—that experienced seducer of the play-writing mind—is mostly very good. This, as I tried to say last night, is not enough. Your first act is over long and is moving in at least two directions at the same time and slowly at that. Act Two is the best, I think, but the scene between Michael and Linda is too drawn out and not conclusive enough to make a high point just before the interval. Act Three is all of twenty minutes too short and yet seems to be devoted to tying up all kinds of loose ends, many of which could have been left to the imagination. Planning, Chris. You must have it or, dramatically, you're dead before you start.

Your characters talk well but only Shaw has managed to get away with this. WHAT IS THE STORY OF 'THE REPROBATE'? Try to answer this in a three line synopsis. If you can—and I certainly can't—then ask yourself whether the content will compel the attention of an audience that is there only to shelter from the rain.

This is your first. Write another twenty and then tear every one up that doesn't conform to the above tiresome but necessary standard.

Enjoyed our evening—said you would get a frank opinion. I hope we are still friends . . .

Paul

Christopher asked the stage doorman where the nearest off licence was. Then he went out and bought a bottle of whisky.

"Not going to down that before the show, old Chris?" Basil had met him on the way in.

"No. After".

"Something wrong?"

"Only my play. Paul blew it sky high and he's absolutely right".

"So. Get stinko and write another".

"For tonight I shall just get stinko".

Basil went into his dressing-room on the ground floor and Christopher climbed the stairs. He knocked on Jackie's door.

"Who is it?"

"Me, Chris".

"Come in . . ."

He went in and felt again a surge of pity for the fact that, while some actors—he, in this piece—have it easy, others have it the hardest. Poor Jackie was standing in bra and pants and held in her hand a sponge that dripped a brown liquid. Her legs and arms were brown, the rest of her body white. She shivered and looked so miserable that he wanted to take her in his arms. But the brown was still wet.

"This bloody stuff's too dark" she was saying. "I shall never get it right".

"Need help?"

"Pauline, my understudy, usually does my back but she isn't in".

"I'm willing, if it's all right with you".

"You'll have to brush very lightly and get it smooth . . . Here".

He took the sponge and Jackie, her back to him, undid her bra and let the shoulder straps fall. Holding the bra against her with one hand, she lifted her back hair and held it on top of her head with the other. It was all Christopher could do to comply efficiently.

Gently he drew the sponge across her shoulders and down her back. As he reached her lower back she said . . . "Get it well down".

"I . . . er . . ."

"It has to go below the level of my bikini, pull my pants down a bit. I can't, I've got my hands full".

They laughed, nervously, at this and Jackie said . . . "Watch it, now. Or, rather, don't".

"If I don't watch how can I see?"

He eased down her pants to what he thought might be

72

the required level and sponged across the top of her buttocks.

"Is it smooth?"

"Looks like silk to me" he said.

"Don't be a bloody fool. I mean the colour".

"That's what I mean, what did you think I meant? There".

He handed her the sponge and she nodded towards the bowl of liquid. "Put it in there, I'm stuck".

He thought how vulnerable she looked, holding the hair with her right hand, the bra with her left.

"It doesn't take long to dry. You wouldn't be an angel and light me a cigarette?"

He lit it and held it out to her. She opened her lips to receive it. She had made up her face but had not yet put on lipstick. Before receiving the cigarette, she received a kiss from him. The lips were cold but moist and exciting. She puffed at the cigarette and he removed it and set it on an ash-tray.

"It's freezing in this room" she said.

"Poor darling. Won't be long. There's a roaring fire waiting for us at home".

"And a roast?"

"I shouldn't wonder" he said.

CHAPTER

10

Christopher waited in the parlour by the fire while Jackie bathed away her sun tan in the upstairs bathroom. He had told her, on the bus ride back, about his play and Paul's letter and they had agreed to down a deal of whisky in uncelebration. He had quite a start on her when she appeared

—in robe again—and he poured her a generous whack while Mrs. Tuffnell brought in supper. The meal took nearly an hour and, by the time Mrs. Tuffnell's offer of tea had been declined—they wouldn't have said "No" to coffee but didn't like to risk her possible disappointment at not having any—and the landlady had said her fond goodnight, they were aglow with food, whisky and fire comfort. He went to the drawer of the sideboard and brought out Mrs. T's leather bound tome.

"History" he announced.

They opened the book on the table and drew their chairs together to sit. Every name in *Who's Who*, it seemed, had made stay under this roof. The earliest date was 1919— the first post war year, in which Mrs. Tuffnell, widow of Sergeant Tuffnell R.E.s (his picture was over the mantel) had refused to submit to sorrow and had begun taking in lodgers. The first entry—following 'By hook or by crook I'll be first in this book, Aunt Effie, (who had given her the volume) . . . '*Both* back from the wars, Leslie Henson'.

"I've heard of him" said Jackie.

Other names, unheard of by either of them, crowded the early pages. Until one page. A blank for the date—1921— and one signature scrawled at the top . . . 'Marie Lloyd' . . .

"Nobody else signed the page" Chris said, in awe. And turned over. More famous unknowns—to them. Then came Melville Gideon, Betty Chester, Laddie Cliff . . . Their signatures were bracketed and one word was written beside the bracket . . . 'Co-Optimistically . . .'

"I've heard of them, too" said Jackie. "The Co-optimists" I mean. My father saw them . . . " 'Owen Nares', 'Fay Compton' . . . 'Carl Brisson', 'Tilly Brisson' . . . 'Jack Buchanan' . . ."

"I've heard of him" said Chris, proudly. "Fay Compton too . . ."

" 'Marie Tempest' . . ." Jackie read.

"Yes" said Chris and read on, trying to sound informed . . . " 'Stanley Lupino' . . . 'Laddie Cliff' again . . . 'José Collins' . . ."

" 'Ivor Novello' " Jackie said.

74

Some signatures were unreadable. Sometimes the artist included the name of the play or musical comedy . . . *'Yes Madam'* they read and Jackie said the tiny, spidery signature must be 'Bobby Howes'. Another, from the title—*Private Lives,* they identified as 'Noel Coward' . . .

"All eating Mrs. Tuffnell's roasts" said Christopher. "It's no wonder they stayed the course".

They were into the thirties now and many names appeared for the second, third or fourth time . . . 'Gertrude Lawrence' was a newcomer, she wrote: 'This time I *did* get in before N.C.!'

" 'Noel Coward' I'll bet he regretted giving her his tour list" said Christopher. He realised how grateful he should be to Basil. He was sure—from the fact that there were still vacant rooms—that Mrs. Tuffnell was selective and you needed to be recommended. He was equally sure that several of the company of *Lady in the Sun* must have written and had polite refusals. Did Basil mind his having recommended Mrs. T. to Jackie—or Jackie to her, which? He knew that, in future, he would be as jealous as the stars of rare addresses like these.

"Here's Basil" said Chris. "And here again . . ."

"There's Paul" Jackie said, as they came to the entry he had seen the night before.

He continued to turn the pages and pore over them, not noticing that Jackie had left the table.

" 'Jack Benny' " he announced, suddenly. "1952 . . ." He turned when there was no reaction. Jackie was stretched out on the rug before the dying fire. She was fast asleep.

Nightly—and at matinees—Chris helped with the sponging. Pauline had found them at it and had given a little whimper and gone.

"It'll be all over the company" said Jackie. "That prissy little virgin can't keep her mouth shut about anything. Especially when it looks like something she never had".

"It isn't though, is it?"

He had got to the lower section of the back and was wondering how long he would endure partly pulling down

75

the pants of one of whom he had never pulled down the pants fully.

"I doubt if Pauline has stood damn nearly starkers in front of a man. But if you were referring to the fact that you are not actually laying me, I agree it isn't".

"You're very firm".

"So are you, I can see, and this is neither the time nor place. Light me a cigarette".

He carried out the routine and went back to spongeing, pulling the pants a little farther down than necessary . . .

"Hey!"

"It's only a bottom, what's a bottom?" As a matter of fact, he admitted to himself, it wasn't. It was quite perfect and special.

"Can't you wait until after the play?"

"I have done, every night, and it's Friday".

"My God, you infant . . ." (Twice in a week? Infant?) "Nature has been biding its time".

A light crashed clumsily on and, by way of elated apology, he kissed the perfection, handed her the sponge and exit.

They sat down to supper at once on coming home. Jackie in shirt and trousers, she would bathe much later, she was hungry. They ate, as the young do, enough to make older folk pale with jealousy. Here was an unnatural imbalance if you liked, the middle-aged are hungry as the young, why did later eating go at once to pot? Or it the pot nature?

"Is there any whisky left?" she asked.

"I bought another bottle this morning".

"I'll go halves".

"All right".

"Infant" she said again.

"Not so much of that. How old are you?"

"Twenty eight. How old are you?"

"Twenty two".

"When?"

"What?"

"When were you twenty two".

"I'm not, but I will be soon".

"Infant".

They sat, he in an armchair, she at his feet, looking into the fire. He kissed her hair.

"It's like wire, isn't it?" she asked.

"Yes".

"Do you always tell the truth?"

"Didn't you want a frank opinion?"

"Of course".

" 'Of course' is meaningless, nobody wants a frank opinion".

"You've discovered?"

"Tuesday night. Or, to be exact, Wednesday evening".

She turned, in inquiry, and he kissed her lips at some length. He tried to slide his hand down the front of her shirt but it stuck on the body paint.

"I bought a new Swedish bath oil today" she said. "Shall we try it out?"

Mrs. Tuffnell slept downstairs at the back of the house, they knew. Jackie ran the bath and both retired to their rooms to undress. He heard her turn off the bath. Then she tapped lightly at his door.

"Want to help?"

She had taken off her make-up and looked younger. A shower cap covered the dyed hair.

They tiptoed to the bathroom at the end of the passage and went in. Jackie locked the door behind them. Christopher was wearing a dressing-gown only and she her white robe. They kissed and he opened the robe. Her perfect little body with the impudent breasts was sadly unlovely with its brown streakings. She took the robe off and got quickly into the bath. The water was thick with the new foam and she slid down so that only her face was visible.

"It's gorgeous" she whispered. "They said in the shop that everything melts away and you're left smooth and lovely. Look!" Already, the brown make-up was being drawn down into the bubbles.

"I forgot my wash bag".

"I'll get it".

"No. Don't. Rub me with your hands, you don't need soap with this".

She knelt up, cupping her breasts. Her body was covered with the rich lather and he was able to stroke away the make-up from her chest and shoulders.

"Do my tummy".

Using both hands, he rubbed her, front and back. Her buttocks. She sat back, suddenly.

"I can do my legs . . ."

But they did them together. Christopher wondered, fleetingly, what would happen if Mrs. T. knocked on the door but he didn't think she would. Jackie knelt up again. She was rubbing gently at her upper thighs. His decision to give assistance here brought a little squeal from her and she sat back again.

"Why don't you go to my room?" she panted. "Give me ten minutes?" Something in his look made her add, hastily . . . "I can manage now. I really can".

Their love making was of a kind new to Christopher. Or was it the intensity that was new? Not entirely. The impersonal nature of it was newer, he wasn't sure that it mattered too much that he was Christopher. It seemed to be more important that he was young and strong at these moments and ready to give more than he took. Jackie was great at taking.

"Run your hands over me, all of me, more, more . . ."

Even the most experienced of his student lovers—Drama student lovers—had wanted to relax in his arms afterwards. The deflowerees clung like convolvulus. When he held Jackie in his arms the merest touch of their skins together fired her to new exploits. It was daylight before they slept. Or would have, Christopher knew that if he closed his eyes the next time they opened would be to behold Mrs. T.

"Where are you going?"

"Back to my own room. I shall probably sleep through to lunch. It's been nice knowing you . . ." He smiled a ghastly smile that was meant to have, at least, some love in it. Exhaustion made his lips cling to his teeth. He was standing naked beside her bed and Jackie reached out a hand to touch him.

"It's beautiful" she said.

To Christopher's astonishment — and somewhat pride — his penis began to rear up. "Do leave it alone" he said. "We have a matinee".

Christopher had heard about nyphomaniacs and knew that he had now met one. She took him in the dressing-room before spongeing . . . It was only the necessity for careful application of the liquid that made her refrain during it. She stood naked now and he sponged without limit. She was on stage quite often during the play but had one wait of about three quarters of an hour and came at once to his room . . . He found it incredibly exciting to have this gorgeous little creature enter, in her attractive facial make-up, lock the door behind her and stand in submission for him to peel off her bikini. The wait occurred before his scene and, one night, he missed his entrance. He received a reprimand from the stage management and walked off after the final calls to glares from the two female stars and a sad look from the male.

"Better come in for a moment" Basil grunted to him as they reached his floor. Inside the dressing-room, Basil's frown changed to a comedy look of bewilderment. "You oversexed or what, old thing?"

"I don't think so. I'm most terribly sorry".

"That's all right, not everybody can be oversexed".

"I mean about missing my entrance. It was unforgiveable".

"It happens to us all. Though, I'm bound to say, not often for the same reason. Christ, the play only lasts for two and a half hours, can't you save your fucking till you get home?"

"*I* can, yes . . ."

"Ah. Say no more. Have a drink".

"Basil . . . How did you know? What I was doing, I mean?"

"How did I know? The bloody theatre's been rocking like

79

a boat for a week, what do you mean how do I know, we *all* know!"

"Shit".

"Exactly. Soda? Not much, I bet . . .?"

"No".

"No. Here".

They drank in silence, then Basil said . . . "It's Thursday . . ."

"Yes" moaned Christopher.

"What? Don't tell me she does you twice on matinee days?"

"At least".

Basil gave a low whistle. "My dear old son. Sit down. What I was about to say was that, it being Thursday, we have only tomorrow and Saturday—another matinee, of course . . ."

Christopher winced as Basil continued . . . "On Sunday we move to Glasgow. Where's she staying in Glasgow?"

"She did give me the address, I've forgotten".

"Oh, that's good. You didn't give her Mrs. MacGregor . . . ?

"No! I say, I wouldn't do that! You and Cecily . . . and you gave me Mrs. MacGregor, I wouldn't do that".

"You gave her Mrs. Tuffnell".

"I was sorry for her. I'm sorry if I did the wrong thing".

"Stop being so sorry. Just don't throw the old digs list around, we like to keep it special. If it isn't an indelicate question where are you going to be doing it next week?"

"Not at Mrs. MacGregor's, I promise you".

"That's all right then. Not that Mrs. MacGregor's a prude. I've bashed the odd female Thespian there in my time but your problem is different. Besides, I've been looking forward to a few chats. Cecily goes to bed early, I like to turn in around two. But I suppose you'll be on the tiles?"

Christopher smiled. "I can't be, can I? I'm staying with you, aren't I and I have to be on my good behaviour".

"That going to be your story?"

"Yes".

"I hope it holds up. Your story, I mean. Of course, she'll be on you like a female agent the moment you set foot in the theatre. Except that she'll take more than ten per cent. None of my business, old banana, but save a little something for tomorrow".

"I'll try. I'd better go now and apologise to the others".

"I wouldn't do that. The mood they're in tonight, they're liable to cut your cock off. Write little notes. Surprising in this profession how people like getting little notes".

"I'm dreading going home tonight".

"Can't help you there, old lad. As far as Mrs. T.'s is concerned, you've made your bed and you must bounce up and down on it".

In the middle of the first night at Glasgow Christopher came bounding into Basil's room.

"She's leaving!"

"Who is?"

"Jackie. She's being released at the end of the week to go into one of Sookie's new productions, she's being replaced".

"Bloody Hell".

"What do you mean? It's marvellous!"

"Try to forget your appendage for a moment. Tell me, who takes over?"

"I don't know. I imagine they'll send somebody up from London".

"And, meanwhile . . .?"

"The understudy?"

"That means rehearsals. And more rehearsals when the new girl joins us, we shall be at it day and night. All because you've been at it day and night".

"What do you mean?"

"Mean? It sticks out a mile, if you'll forgive the phrase. Sookie's releasing her because he doesn't want you to get too used to doing it the right way round. Have you had your week-end invitation, by the by?"

"No".

"You will".

"You can't be serious. You mean Sookie knows?"

"Nothing goes on in a Lamont production that doesn't

81

get reported to Sookie. He knew about it before you took it out".

"Act Two, beginners . . ." said the Tannoy. Basil put his cigarette out and got into his jacket. He believed in cutting costume changes down to the minimum. (Come on in a different suit and they spend five minutes wondering who the hell you are".)

"You'd better get back upstairs, make the most of your time" he said. Christopher's face fell.

"Now, now . . ." said Basil, touching the end of his nose with a damp chamois leather. "Service with a smile!"

"Service with a smile".

Christopher smiled at the memory and looked up at the same moment. Another voice had spoken. He continued to smile at the owner of the voice but the smile was polite now, no longer expressive of amusement. His fellow traveller stood in the doorway of the compartment, holding coffee in a disposable cup.

"It was good of you, thank you".

"I don't know whether that's white enough, it's the way I drink it. And I don't take sugar, do you?" He held out the little green packet of two cubes.

"No".

"Some biscuits, if you'd like them?"

Another extension of the delicate hand. Christopher took the biscuits, smiling again. He was irked that the homo had brought him just the refreshment he had refrained from asking for. He would resent enjoying it. The hell. Drink up and eat, he makes you feel uncomfortable by his presence, draw compensation from his coffee and biscuits. Christopher wondered whether you got nymphomaniac homos. And whether the degree of nymphomania stepped up or down the tempo of the ocular dance.

He set his coffee on the little stand to his left and opened the packet of biscuits. Noisily. As though to make any kind of delicate movement would draw him on to common ground with the fawn man.

"I'm Dorian Gray . . ."

"Er . . ."

"Like the character in the book, it's too amusing, isn't it? I might have changed it. My name. But I really didn't see why I should. I hope it's the only similarity".

"I'm . . . Christopher Tighson".

"How do you do?"

Christopher dreaded a meeting of their hands but Gray forebore to offer. A very careful Gray. He was speaking.

"You mustn't feel that, because we are now properly introduced, you have to drop your work and engage me in conversation . . ."

It was as though he expected you to side-step him and would always side-step first to avoid even the hint of a slight.

"It's . . . something I've written, I really should finish checking it before I get to London . . ."

"Not another word!"

Gray seemed to curl up like an ageing pixie behind his newspaper. He crossed one leg over the other and, out of the corner of his eye, Christopher could see one pointed toe, jigging . . .

Glasgow passed and so did Jackie. Basil's hoped for nocturnal chats didn't materialise because he was worried about Christopher's health.

"Straight to bed, build up. There's time. We're bound to stop rehearsing one of these days".

"We're not rehearsing tomorrow".

"Some of us may be performing though. Goodnight".

Jackie was clearly frustrated but the thought of her new part—a more rewarding one, theatrically—did something to help.

"I could still turn it down. I haven't signed".

"No!" said Christopher and had to temper the vehemence of the negative . . . "Sookie would never forgive you and you know how he is".

"I know how I am. We haven't slept together for nearly a week".

"It's four days . . ."

"I'm coming to your room tonight in the break".

"No!"

"Why not? You don't want me any more, that's what it is".

"I want you too much. It's just that if I miss my entrance again I shall get the sack".

"Then you could come to London with me".

"And never work again?"

"Come back to my digs after the show".

"I can't do that. Mrs. Macgregor's very strict about meals".

"Tell her you're going out".

"Who with, Basil will want to know. Whom do I know in Glasgow?"

"Me".

"You were the reason I missed my entrance and he hasn't forgiven us" he lied.

Suddenly Christopher wondered why he was making these difficulties. Basil's insistence upon early nights, Mrs MacGregor's food and his own avoiding tactics in the theatre had laid in a stock for him.

"Is your landlady broad minded?"

"I haven't tried her. As you well know".

"How about tomorrow afternoon? Tea?"

"I don't know about tea" she said.

Tomorrow was Friday and they celebrated goodbye. He avoided an encore that evening and the next day was conveniently cluttered with a matinee and with packing. On Sunday morning, on her own lonely train call . . . Jackie passed.

The understudy opened in Edinburgh and a pale, Lamont style understudy she turned out to be. A friend of Miss Cowles? Liane arrived on the Monday in time to watch the play and begin rehearsals next morning. She was a lush brunette—who had refused to dye her hair, last minute casting always gave the actor an edge, she said 'No' to peroxide and the 'No' was accepted. They rehearsed daily. And plainly Liane was going to be better than Jackie which calmed the stars and took away from Christopher's remorse.

"Give it time before you start on this one, old Chris", Basil had said.

Christopher was enjoying Edinburgh. Since rehearsals didn't always involve him, he managed a trip to the castle. He had long been fascinated by the known and unknown factors of the Mary Queen of Scots story and was furious with the guide who ruined the visit for him by including cheap jokes in his patter. Mrs. Grant was one more on the rare list and good food—but why did the Scots over-cook their beef?—and a flaming hearth made home. Late night chats had to be foregone again in favour of sleep before early rehearsals. . . .

"She's going to be good, though" said Christopher.

"She'd better be".

Liane was due to join the play a week after her first arrival—in Aberdeen. She was a quick study and it was important to get her 'played in'. They had St. John Pender —extracting his own chestnuts with tongs already to hand. Christopher had expected Sookie but he never travelled so far north. Paul? He had written to thank Paul for his detailed analysis of *The Reprobate* but had received no answer. None was called for, though. They journeyed to Aberdeen on the Sunday and spent most of Monday in the theatre, dress rehearsing. Only Liane was in costume and make-up. But they ran the whole play to allow her to become accustomed to the waits. One hour's rest before curtain up but, then, the by now accepted Bannerman success. They were a sell-out at all performances—sometimes before they arrived in a city.

"'You're being spoilt, young Chris" Basil said. "You

don't know what it is to raise a laugh from a half-empty house". He added, sadly, "You will, though".

Liane had done well and was well noticed. At last, they were going to be able to relax in the daytimes, see something of the cities and the countryside around and indulge in the luxury of the late, fireside conversation.

Two events occurred to further Christopher's sex education this tour. Despite Basil's injunction to him to keep off, he began to fancy Liane. The stimulus of the first three weeks in the tour had stepped up his physical renewal. The body, it seemed, when left for a period without sex, would adjust to stagnation point. Over stimulated, it would tend to say—after the first surprise—"All right, all right. Now we are tuned and the fuel is flowing regularly into the tank, up with the mileage". Thereafter, it was difficult to come down again to a low gear trundle. And he fancied Liane. She was taller than Jackie but beautifully built. Large, green eyes and bone structure for the face. For the rest, a small but enticing bosom, no bottom at all and long, shapely legs. Her mouth, an over large slash full of promise. The night after her opening in Aberdeen, he tapped gently at her door on his way up. He heard something which he took to be an invitation to enter. He opened the door to see Liane—in the familiar bra and pants, already sponged brown. Pauline was there, facing the mirror on the dressing-table. She was stripped to the waist and very bulbous and pink too. Liane stood behind her, her hands caressing the pink-tipped bulbs of Pauline, both looking intently into the mirror and, clearly, in another world of enjoyment.

Christopher closed the door quietly and stood for a moment of dazed incredulity. Then he leapt down the stairs and knocked on Basil's door.

"Enter".

"Basil. Liane . . ."

"Yes?"

"She's a lesbian".

"Of course she is, so's Pauline or hadn't you noticed?"

"No" Chris said.

"Well you live and learn, don't you, old sort? Have to shove it in cotton wool till we get back to London".

As a preliminary to the second event, Basil threw a log on the fire, poured liberally from the whisky bottle for them both, and conservatively from the water jug.

"It's a rum thing, nature" he said.

"Yes".

Mrs. Grant had retired early, Cecily had kissed and departed and a whole philosophical field lay before them to be ploughed and sown.

"Here's to nature . . ."

"Nature" Christopher said.

They drank and Basil eased his bottom to comfort in a deep chair. "Take this girl Liane . . ."

"She's good, isn't she?"

"Stop salving your conscience, of course she's good. That doesn't alter the fact that we've been rehearsing our arses off. What was I saying?"

"Take this girl Liane".

"Yes. Beautiful. Strips like a dream. And what does she do with it? Rubs it up against another female, goes in for acrobatics. What I ask myself is, given a good stallion, could she be won back to stud?"

His gaze pulled away from the fire and shot to Christopher. "I'm not giving *you* ideas, mind!"

"No" said Christopher. And Basil gazed into the fire again.

"I don't think she could, anyway" he said. "Pauline perhaps, yes, but not Liane . . ."

"Pauline?"

"I don't think she' a natural les., she's just frightened of men. Likes to be mothered and, before you can say "Knickers", she's fathered and Liane talks her into doing it the safe way. Mind you, a Lesbian can be exciting in bed—ever come across it?"

"No".

"The ones who can't make up their mind I mean. I must say I'd rather shack up with a girl who's half a man than a man who's half a girl . . ."

"Ever come across that?"

"Male bicycles? Not from personal knowledge, I'm happy to say, but I've come across them. One star I know takes

man woman or Alsatian and not only to get himself a contract. He talks largely about living a brim full sex life and I
think he means it".

"What about . . . ?"

"What about what?"

"Did you . . . have trouble at school?"

"I fell in love with a boy who had fuzz on his cheeks
and long eye lashes but that's because my subconscious
thought he was a girl".

'Did you do anything about it?'

"I wanted to kiss him but when I put my arm round
him in the rugger scrum he smelled of Sharp's Kreamy
Toffee and it put me off".

"Did you . . . get stimulated?"

"Get a cockstand? Sure. We were six of us, packed into
a bath of hot water after the match and I happened to be
next to him. Talk about up periscope!"

Christopher laughed and Basil looked quite surprised.
"Nothing to laugh at, old horseman. It was Nature getting
on with the serious business of boy meets what, for the
moment, has to pass for girl. It never entered my head there
was anything strange. Mind you, I was lucky . . ."

"What do you mean?"

"Homo Jomo. We didn't go in for that at my school. As
such, that is. The result was that, when I went out into the
lascivious world, I had a built in, cast iron cork of innocence. A certain very large star who shall be nameless once
held my hand for half an hour and I thought he was telling
my fortune. He was heard to observe later "Of course, he's
got such a bloody air of virgin purity about him I wouldn't
want him now, anyway". Don't underrate innocence. It's
a great saver for the young of both sexes. Pro tem, of
course. When I finally did learn about Homo Jomery you
could have knocked me down with a jock-strap. Did you get
it at school?"

"Yes and no. One of the boys had a shot at me but it
misfired and they put me through hell. But . . ."

"But what?"

"Never mind".

"All right".

"I . . . I'd like to talk about it . . ."

"Go on, then. What about a drink first?"

"Yes. I say, I haven't stood my whack this week. I can't drink all your whisky".

"Certainly you can't. I shall drink half. Go on".

Basil poured and remained out of Christopher's eyeline while he told the story of the nightmare that was born that day in the changing-room. Having heard it, he brought the glass to Christopher, sat down again and sipped. Then he said . . . "So, what's worrying you?"

"The . . . fact that, twice, I got this erection . . . and I didn't even like the boy".

"You must have liked what he was doing to you".

"Exactly. But in this case I didn't think he was attractive so does that mean I'm a latent queer?"

There was a spluttering. "Christ, I've spilt half my whisky. Look. I don't follow your reasoning. If you'd thought him attractive but regarded him, in your subconscious, as female then what you got would be back-handed nature. If you thought him an attractive *boy,* it still wouldn't make you a queer—especially in the light of your subsequent capers. It would be Nature being perverse, perhaps, but not necessarily perverted. But you saw him as a boy and didn't like him, how does that make you queer?"

"There was no natural reason for the stimulation".

"Look . . ." said Basil again. "Cocks are funny things and they rise for all kinds of—sometimes unaccountable—reasons. Sensitivity—especially to being uncovered . . . Even nudists have trouble and have to go jump in the lake. Good God, when I had my army medical I reared up like a mamba but that didn't mean I wanted to bugger the M.O."

"So . . ."

"So. Not to worry. What's more, if you're queer what the hell have we been doing all this rehearsing for?"

"I think . . . it has affected me".

"Rehearsing or fucking?"

"The business at school. I don't seem to want a girl after the first time. The same one, I mean, I want another".

"You were faithful to Jackie for two weeks".

The period of time was not long but Christopher realised, suddenly, that—apart from the exhaustion aspect—he had, in fact, continued to want Jackie. For the longest time yet. He still wanted her.

"Can I have some more whisky?" he asked.

They talked until the last pourings, then Basil said . . . "Do you know what a woman once told me? We were on the job at the time . . ."

"What?"

"I must prefix this by saying that I used to be pretty adept . . ."

"Yes?"

"She was pleased anyway, and she said did I know what it was made me a good lover and I said "What?" and she said . . . "Because you have more than a touch of the woman in you". What do you make of that?"

Christopher didn't answer and they continued to gaze at the last embers in the grate.

"Rum thing, nature" Basil said. Christopher raised his glass. "Nature" he said.

"Nature . . ."

CHAPTER

12

Given a good stallion, could she be won back to stud? Christopher looked across at D. Gray and wondered if the question would be more or less easily answerable if, for 'stallion', you substituted 'mare' and 'he' for 'she'. It was a mistake because D. Gray took a breath and would have begun speech but for a split-second dive by C. Tighson into his manuscript. The breath came out again as a scented sigh and only the train wheels were heard thereafter.

Christopher Agatha-Christied a slow hand in the direction of his coffee and drew it towards him. The train braked suddenly and he was constrained to take the remainder two thirds of a cup in one gulp or spill. He gasped, put down the cup, coughed and took out a handkerchief, all without raising his head. The pages still unblemished. Except by his words?

Their invitations to Sookie's weekend party reached them next day. Newcastle was to follow. Then Oxford, Sookie gave plenty of notice. They accepted. You didn't turn down an invitation from Sookie whether professional or social. How did you turn down the more personal invitation Christopher knew would come? The rest of the cast knew it would come, too, and most thought it would serve him bloody well right for that scandalous behaviour in Manchester . . .

"At least, the poofs don't do it all over the dressing-room" the male star was heard to say to the female star with talent. "Not to the point of missing entrances . . ." he qualified.

"You're jealous, darling".

"Nothing of the kind".

"Well, I am".

Christopher asked Basil to give him the low-down—if he would overlook the phrase—on the week-end routine.

"We motor over after the play on the Saturday night. I shall go to London from Newcastle, bring the car to Oxford, I'll give you a lift . . ."

"Thank you".

"We arrive soon after midnight and have an entrancing supper with champagne by the silver bucket—he gets it off tax. Thank God it isn't summer otherwise he'd have us all in the pool. Insist on our bathing, I meant to say. We shall probably be made to play games . . ."

"Christ".

"Don't worry, he draws the line at Postman's Knock . . . Around two thirty, we of the normality will retire and there endeth the first chapter. Except . . ."

"Yes?"

"You'll be expected to linger downstairs".

"What for?"

"And we'll be expected not to notice, it's standard with Sookie. Now, all you have to do, in a firm but very subtle manner, is to convey that Homo Jomo is out. Whatever you do—and here's the crux—don't let your host get to the stage of making an actual physical touch. If you turn him down then he'll never speak to you again. Which, of course, is professional near death".

"How do I do it, then?"

"That's up to you".

"Did you go through it with him when you were young?" Basil breathed half way in. "I could have done without the last phrase" he said.

"Sorry".

"Don't mention it. I played the whole thing for comedy. I was playing a peach of a part for him at the time and the sun shone out of my comic arse. It went like this . . .

Sookie: Are you happy in the play?

Me: You mean theatrically or sexually, sir? (I was your age then . . .)

Sookie: Both.

Me: Theatrically, ecstatic—*because* we have all those gorgeous girls, you see. I need girls to make me happy, sexually, and, theatrically, they spur me on. I wish I were queer, sir . . ."

Sookie: (Interested) You do?

Me: Then I wouldn't need the stimulus, queers seem to be able to let go at the drop of a poke bonnet. You must have noticed! (Queers love it if they think you assume they aren't. That's why I kept giving him the "sir".) I think they're wonderful!

Sookie: (Nonplussed) You do?

Me: You're so clever, sir, to employ so many. (All employers like to be reminded that they employ.) I'm glad you employ me too but I could never aspire to being a queer.

Sookie: (No fool) You're pulling my leg, you young bastard . . ."

Me: (Mock humility but funny with it.) That's all I'm good for, sir, to clown. And make love to girls, isn't it ordinary?"

And that, more or less, is how I succeeded in calling my bottom my own. You may have to play it differently . . ."

Jackie's play opened in Brighton the night *Lady in the Sun* opened in Newcastle. The company sent her a joint wire, Christopher adding one of his own. It brought a telephone call to his digs the same night.

"Chris?"

"How did it go?"

"Not too badly. I was a bag of nerves . . ."

"I'll bet you were marvellous".

He had read the script and knew there was no spongeing involved. There was one scene in which she had to undress. He wanted to ask her about this, be reassured that she hadn't to go too far. Why the hell should he care? Jealousy? Of Jackie?

"Two weeks rehearsal is no joke . . ." she was saying. "I just about got through".

She asked about Liane—who had done well with only one week's rehearsal—but Christopher made circumspect reply.

"Miss me?" she asked. Archly, he thought. There were one or two young stag parts in her play and he knew she wouldn't suffer physical deprivation unless she wanted to. He didn't think she did.

"Like hell"—which, as he said it, he realised could mean two things. But he had missed her.

"You didn't answer my last letter".

"I wrote twice".

"Big deal, I wrote three times and I've been rehearsing".

"What do you think I've been doing?"

"Chris . . ." she went on, quietly . . .

"Yes?"

"Can't you get the sleeper to London on Saturday? I can come up . . ."

Here we go, he thought. He was also in a state to be happy at the prospect, he was beginning to eye the female A.S.M. with the glasses. He thought she might have boobs.

"I'll be there".

93

"We can spend all day and night".

Oh, shit.

She went on . . . "We go to Bournemouth next week, you're at Oxford . . ."

He'd told her, but she could have looked it up in The Stage, anyway.

"So, we both leave on Monday morning. All topped up . . ."

He wasn't sure about the expression used. But, desire being a spendthrift, he said . . . I'll be there for breakfast . . ."

He hoped to God she would let him eat it.

Basil and Chris checked their tickets with the sleeping-car attendant. "When it comes to sleeping in a train", Basil had said, "travel First. You won't sleep, anyway, but in First Class at least you have the illusion of a bed". And Christopher had blown the addition to the fare as provided by the management. Cecily had gone to London earlier in the week.

"Do you see what I see?" Christopher asked Basil.

"What?"

"The Les. is travelling".

Liane was following a porter who pushed a trolley load of expensive looking luggage. At her heels on a thick leash, walked a huge, obedient borzoi.

"Liane!"

"Chris. Basil. I thought I wouldn't make it. Like a fool, I left my luggage at the hotel . . ." She opened a handbag the size of a suitcase, rummaged about in it. Basil gave the porter half a crown and winked at Christopher from her blind side.

"All done".

"What? Oh, you are kind. This is Serge".

"I didn't know you had a dog" said Christopher.

"He isn't a dog, he's a White Russian".

"You could have fooled me" said Basil. "You've been holding out on us".

94

"I always keep him at the hotel. He doesn't like the theatre".

"Wise White Russian" said Basil. "Baggage is aboard, we're holding up the traffic . . . After you, Serge . . ."

Liane undid the leash and Serge walked into the train.

Basil announced that he had a half bottle of Scotch and invited them to join him for a nightcap.

"What about Serge?" he said to Liane. "Does he drink Scotch?"

Serge stalked ahead of them and, at a word from Liane, paused outside a door.

"Number Ten" she said. "That's us Serge. In". Serge strode into the compartment and, obviously used to and contemptuous of confined spaces, executed a solemn turn by putting his fore-legs on the bunk, landing at last in a position facing the door.

"Sit".

He sat.

"Down"

The commands were quietly spoken, so as not to appear commands at all. With a gentle thud Serge dropped into a lying position, filling most of the floor space.

"How will you get into bed?" Basil asked.

"First things first. You mentioned a nightcap. I'll bring Serge his in a saucer".

"You mean he does drink Scotch?"

"You invited him".

"But of course".

"He eats and drinks whatever I eat and drink. I wouldn't feel happy otherwise".

Basil waved a weak hand at Serge and they moved on to Number Twelve, Christopher pausing at Eleven to drop his suitcase.

As has been said of whisky, one (person)—in a sleeper— is all right. Two is too many and three is not enough. When you get three, you might as well have the Marx Brothers and all, nobody is comfortable. They perched on the bunk and Basil produced the half bottle and a set of metal cups that fitted one into another for travelling.

"Anybody mind it neat?"

95

Nobody did.

"Oxford, Brighton . . ." he said, filling the cups, ". . . and then London. Here's hoping we get a year".

"Or two" Liane said.

"Settle for eighteen months, let's not be greedy".

The attendant stood at the open door.

"Early morning tea?" he asked.

"What time do we get in?" asked Basil.

"Five o'clock".

"There's no such time."

"You can stay in your compartment until six-thirty, you won't be disturbed".

"I don't think I want early morning tea, do you?" Basil asked the others and they said "No". "What about Serge? No? No, thank you" he said to the attendant.

"Goodnight, all. Sleep well."

"I doubt if I shall sleep at all" said Basil. "Unless this helps".

They half lay back on the bunk and drew hopefully upon the Scotch for assistance. Liane proved to be a compulsive talker. She was mannish but very desirable, Christopher thought Now what the hell did that make you, if you lusted after a Lesbian? She talked about the theatre and the kickings of new life within it. She wondered how long light comedies would continue to attract . . .

"You said two years".

"Paul Bannerman is in a class by himself. *Lady in the Sun* is the best thing he's ever done".

"In the comedy line" said Basil.

"I didn't know he ever wrote anything else."

"His first play, *Galatea*, wasn't a comedy" said Christopher.

"No" said Basil. "And that was his best, in my view".

"I never saw it".

"You wouldn't have. You and Chris weren't born when he wrote it. Or, if you were, you weren't taking notice".

"Did it run?"

"No".

"Why not? Wait a minute, *Galatea* . . . Wasn't that the Susan Chase play?"

"You could say so".

"Did you know her?"

"Very well. In a way. In another way, nobody knew her. What about giving Serge a shot of whisky, may I watch?"

The subject so changed, they trooped to Number Ten and the ceremony took place. Serge lapped up an easy double.

"He isn't getting any more" said Basil, firmly. And they returned to Twelve to finish off the half.

"If I'd known we were going to have a White Russian aboard" he said, "I'd have brought Vodka. I'm happy to say the trifle of Scotch has made me sleepy. It won't last, I know from experience, but I shall now wish you good-night and gave it the usual try. See you at six bloody thirty . . ."

Christopher got into bed, his brain outstripping the fast rhythm of the wheels. *Galatea* he intended to buy. And to read, as being the first of Paul's writing, the one not subject to Euclyd. And he wanted to learn more from Basil about the Paul Bannerman Susan Chase story. He would read that up too, in the library at Oxford—would they have back numbers of newspapers? Or in Fleet Street when they got to London, surely there was a way? He was already acknowledging to himself that Basil would not be readily communicative . . .

There came a tap on his door and Liane entered without waiting for his answer to it, closing the door behind her.

"I found another half bottle. Actually, I didn't find it, I knew I had packed it but I forgot about it".

"You didn't want to share it".

"No, you're right, I didn't. Was it mean?"

"Yes. You might at least have watered the bloody dog".

"He isn't a bloody dog . . ."

"I know, he's a bloody White Russian. And I can see right through whatever it is you're wearing".

"That's better. May I sit down?"

"Be my house guest".

She collected his tooth glass from its holder—she had

97

brought her own, he saw—and came to sit on the bunk.
Chris sat up and watched her with growing interest.

"Aren't you cold?"

"Of course".

She wore no dressing-gown, had travelled from next door
in a nightdress that showed everything in the dim reading-
light he had left on. Her near nakedness seemed to mean
nothing to her. She poured the whisky.

"You'd better put my coat on, you'll freeze".

"If you take off those pyjamas, I won't. Nor will you.
Good health".

"Good health".

They drank.

"Well?"

"Well what?"

"Aren't you going to take them off?"

"I thought you were queer" he said, looking straight
into her eyes. Up to now, he had been looking everywhere
but.

"You've got a bloody nerve. I thought *you* were, anyway".

He was glad he had finished taking his second swallow
of Scotch. "Me?"

"Pauline said you were".

"Pauline! Christ. That must have been because she fancied you . . . I happened to walk in, you know . . ."

"I knew you did. She has a nice body, I like to handle
nice things".

"If you thought I was queer, what are you doing in my
compartment?"

"Drinking whisky".

"And asking me to strip?"

"I told you. I like to handle nice things".

A sleeper bunk is not the most suitable place in which
to indulge in free-for-all sex. Liane managed with surprising dexterity. It was an experience, again, new to him
and by no means wholly satisfying. She took the initiative,
stripping him and feeling his body with large, firm hands.
It occurred to him—and, much as she aroused wanting in
him, he was able to assess this quite objectively as she

98

caressed him— that this was Jackie in reverse. Every demand Jackie had made from him in manual titillation Liane pressed on him, undemanded. He tried to take off her nightdress, caress her, but she forestalled him by making his senses leap in ways that were, as yet, barely acceptable to him. Her lingual expertise caused him to arch his body, half in ectasy, half in disgust.

"There's no room on this bloody bunk" she said, after one manoeuvre.

"There is if you do it like this" he said. He tore down the front of her nightdress and pulled it away from her body. She fought him when he tried to kiss her, digging her fingernails into his flesh.

"You bitch" he said, and grasped her hands, forcing them above her head. "You want everything your own way, don't you? You think you're a bloody man. I have news for you. Men don't have these".

She fought again as he tried to enter her body. Suddenly, Christopher slapped her, hard, across the face. For a mement, she lay stunned. with surprise more than by the blow, and during the moment he entered her. He expected immediate resistance but she lay, submissive. She gave a faintly audible moan when he was fully inside her and began to respond, no longer as a male but as a desirable, desiring female, receiving, giving. She gave with complete abandon, once he had to put a hand over her mouth to prevent her crying out. Never did she look at him. Her eyes tight closed, her head turned to one side. As she reached her peak she began to jerk her head back and forth on the pillow in an ever quickening rhythmic rejection-in-acceptance. Her performance drew from Christopher new efforts—and achievements—in discovery. He could feel the neck of her womb and passed from one side to another of it. Deeper. Her orgasm was long and he was barely able to outstay her. Her head continued to beat on the pillow as he released and was drained by her to the utmost. At last, she opened her eyes and looked into his. She was crying and the look held frank hostility. She pushed him away from her and looked down at their jointure with disgust. Almost with a snarl, she jerked her lower body from his and, thrusting him aside, slid to the floor.

"You bastard" he heard her say. She found the door, opened it noisily, stumbled through it, banging it shut after her.

Christopher went into a deep sleep and came to life only when the train stopped. He pulled aside the blind and saw that it was an intermediate halt. Lights were on on the platform and there was even some movement. He saw Liane, too. Wearing a fur coat—over nakedness, he suspected. She was walking the dog.

"Jesus" he said, aloud. She might have been strolling down Bond Street, her poise, the leash, the disdain of Serge. He watched her as she came along the platform. When she was within a few feet of his window she saw him. Or looked at him, must have seen him. But her eyes moved past him without flinching, without show of recognition. It was a complete cut-dead. On Crewe Station in the middle of the night and she had just balled the Hell out of him. He sat back on the bunk, chucked a pillow in the air and shook with laughter.

As he left the train at King's Cross—no sign of Liane—Christopher saw Basil.

"Share a taxi?"

"I'm going to St. John's Wood . . ."

"Are you, now? Better get one of your own. Where's Liane?"

"Went off early, I suppose".

As they walked along to the taxi rank . . . "Basil?"

"Yes?"

"You were wrong about one thing . . ."

13

Jackie greeted him at her door, wearing a housecoat. He smelt coffee. She touched the underneath of his eyes . . .

"You poor darling. Was it a dreadful journey?"

"It was bumpy".

"Did you get any sleep at all?"

"Some. How goes the play?"

"All right, I think. How's yours?"

"Harry Packers".

"We're Harry Packers too but Brighton is a small theatre. And the town if full of pros., most of 'em poofs. They all thought it was the greatest".

"Would you mind if I had a bath?"

"Darling. This is the beginning of a short but luxurious weekend. I'll cook the eggs and bacon while you clean up, you can use my Swedish oil".

"Over the swish-in of the bath water . . . "You still use it then?"

"Wouldn't be without it. But thank God I don't brown up in this play . . ."

"You strip down, though".

"Sort of".

"How far?"

"What's it to you?"

"I don't know" said Chris, and didn't. "What are the men like?"

"The young? One queer, one womaniser. But he doesn't 'ise' me".

"You mean you haven't . . . since . . .?"

"Don't ask questions you mightn't like to hear the answer to. Have you?"

"Can I have coffee in the bath?"

"You mean in the water?"

She kissed him and he drank deeply from it.

"Hey!"

"Well, it's nice to be kissed by a woman".

"What have you been up to?" she asked but went off at once to the kitchen.

He got into the bath and sighed loudly for her to hear as he lay down in the warm lather. Only his head was visible. Jackie brought coffee, setting the cup and saucer precariously on the soap rack.

"Sit up and I'll do for you what you did for me".

"Let me soak a bit. When do you think your play will come in?"

"A few weeks yet. No theatre. But that won't bother Sookie, he'll whip off something that isn't his and happens to be struggling. *Cloth of Gold*, probably".

"I saw it while we were rehearsing. It's a marvellous play".

"It's also in one of Sookie's theatres and their break figure is astronomical".

"What does that mean?"

"Break figure? Don't you know? It's the takings figure they can't go below for more than two weeks in a row without being shown the door".

"You mean they won't nurse it?"

"The management would, after those notices they'd be crazy not to. But if Sookie wants the theatre for us and they fall below his break figure, they're out and we're in. We're not as good a play but we have stars. Wash your back?"

Christopher sat up in the bath and she sponged his back with slow, loving movements that had a rhythm familiar to them both. Their eyes met, in recognition of the fact. Suddenly she stopped.

"What the hell . . . ?"

"What?"

"What are all these scratches on your back?"

"Scratches?"

"Scratches, yes. Don't tell me Sookie heard about us?"

"He did, I think . . ."

"And met you at the train and clawed you before you got up?"

"What do you mean?"

"You know damn well what I mean, those scratches are new. Last night new. Who did you travel down with?"

"With whom" he corrected, lightly.

"Grammar, my arse" she said. "Who—whom—did you fuck last night that either didn't like it or liked the hell out of it?"

"I travelled down with Basil".

"Who's as queer as Errol Flynn, who else?"

"Don't ask questions you mightn't like to hear the answer to".

She made a wide swipe at him with the sponge, knocking the coffee cup and saucer into the bath.

"Jackie!"

"I don't want to know. And I had such plans . . ."

Christopher never did learn what they were. She rushed out of the bathroom and came back bringing his suitcase and his clothes which she flung on the floor.

"Out" she said.

"Jackie . . ."

"Out!"

"But . . . the eggs and bacon . . ."

"That's all you can think of, feeding Number One . . ."

"What about you?"

"What?"

"There are more ways of feeding than off eggs and bacon" he said, and stood up in the bath to gain an advantage. Jackie was devoid of answer, looking though.

"You . . . you . . ." she said. And left him.

The water in the bath had turned a very ugly shade.

He sat down in the strange mixture of liquids and completed his ablutions at leisure. At one point he sang. What was one cup of coffee in so much Swedish oil? He dried himself at leisure too, dressed at leisure. Then he sallied forth. He found that he was walking on tip-toe. He saw Jackie's back in the kitchen as he left the sitting-room but it wasn't until he had opened the front door fully that he called . . .

"Goodbye!"

Before she could answer, or look round, he was on the other side of the door and heading for the street. He was happy—not ecstatically, but happy—about all the morning's events so far. Except for the breakfast.

The building wasn't expecting him.

He had had a bath, thank God—he didn't have to cope with that shilling in the slot bit, and in Cornwall Place, S.W. you had to clean the bath before you got into it. If you were fussy. And it seemed he was the only tenant in the building who was. The room hadn't been cleaned, the most you got in the way of service was the removal of your rubbish from outside your door. Unless you made a private arrangement. He was used to cleaning his own quarters but when the tour loomed up he did tackle the woman who sometimes 'helped'. (Leaving, always, the ash that dropped from her cigarette—she never took it from her mouth until it was about to set light to her lip.)

"You never 'ad me before".

"No".

"Always do for yourself, I thought you did".

"I'm going away".

"Lucky you".

To some people it never will occur that others work. He forebore to enlighten her and she went on . . .

" 'Ow long for?"

"Eight weeks".

"You could spread newspaper".

"Couldn't you . . . help me out?"

"I don't mind. It'll cost you twenty-five bob a week".

"Twenty-five . . . ? I thought you charged seventeen and six?"

"That's if it's all year round".

He knew that the rooms took her not more than half an hour apiece, and there were seven tenants—six using her slapdash services. She was paid by the landlord to do the stairs and take down the rubbish. And to clean the bathrooms, he was sure.

"I'll pay you a pound".

"Twenty five bob, take it or leave it".

"I'll leave it".

"Suit yourself".

He had regretted allowing himself the satisfaction. Now, as he opened his door, he regretted again. He had closed the windows, of course, and drawn the curtains but the muck in the air at Cornwall Place needed no opening for entry. It materialised within the very room and settled thick and black upon everything. Damn. Dust sheets. He must get dust sheets, one for his theatre suit too, when you dressed higher up than the stars—stars, in the theatre, are high in billing, low in accommodation—you were wardrobeless and curtainless, just a rail. Newspapers. The old bag was right, he could have covered the room with newspapers, the print was disinfectant, even.

He flung the curtains apart with a savage force that split one of them at the top and tumbled the dust of both into the air. Not adding to the sum total he thought—with calm after the savagery. Merely a swopping of one settling place for another. He unlocked the window, pulling the top one down, throwing up the bottom, skinning his knuckles.

The sun played on to his few belongings, spotlighting the merry dance of the dust that was about to double blanket them. He took off his jacket, bundled it into the wardrobe and set to work. He was appalled to see that his typewriter was uncovered. He had decided to take along his play script and had re-typed some of the scenes. In his excitement at leaving . . . The wretched machine that was, to him, an extension of his thought processes was now muck-covered. Tears stung his eyes and he damned his wastage of precious thinking time over the past weeks.

The clean up became a penance. After a solid hour of grubbing about, he had the room in some slight shape but now felt he did need a bath. He settled for washing his face. Then he remembered he had not broken his fast—Mrs. MacGregor's excellent packed snack long forgotten. His small, fold-up kitchen, larder, what could you call it? . . . contained a few biscuits that had gone soft, sugar that had gone sticky and some remainder modern coffee powder that could only be moved with knife jabs.

"Shit" he said aloud, adding several mental comments of a derogatory nature concerning nymphos, lesbians and animal behaviour. Where the hell did you go for breakfast in London on a Sunday? Telephone his father? Nobody would ever arrive to breakfast there. He looked at the painting by his mother that hung on the drab wall. Trees and open sky and longing. She was gone now and his father was as self-contained as the fold-up kitchen . . .

He took a knife and speared away a lump of coffee from the side of the jar. Theatrically, he upended the jar a foot above a cup and the lump fell, cracking the cup. Not to be taught, he hurled the cup at a bin which fell over, jerking a few dreggy bits and pieces out on to the carpet he had just Ewbanked. He replaced these, using dramatically delicate fingers, covering the bin with exaggerated care. As he got up, he banged his head on a shelf, knocking the instant coffee jar on to the floor. It rolled out of reach under the bed. Just to show it, he left it there, filling the kettle, slowly, plugging it in, preparing another cup, setting it on a saucer . . . Then he took up the knife and approached the bed. He made full use of surprise, swinging the bed aside and grabbing the jar before it had a chance to avoid. Jabbing again with the knife gave him some satisfaction. The kettle boiled and he poured water on to what looked like a knob of iron rust. The telephone bell rang.

The slot telephone was on the floor above and there was little likelihood the call was for him but he ran to answer it. To display his independence to the contents of his fold-up kitchen, more than anything. Of course, it *might* be Jackie . . . Not that he would go back to her, even if she offered roast lamb for lunch. Roast lamb . . .

"Hullo?" he said.

"Who is that?"

This kind of opening from a voice maddened him, weak as he was, still, from battle shock.

"It's me, who are you?"

The voice ascertained that it was connected with the right number, then said . . .

"I wanted to speak with Miss Walker . . ."

"Miss who?"

A whiff of scent caught his nostrils and he looked around. A girl had come out of the room nearby. Fresh faced, red haired, slim waisted. In Sunday sweater and slacks, both items proud of what they were covering.

"Is it for me?"

"Miss Walker?"

"Yes. I moved in two days ago".

Certainly, he hadn't seen her before. And she was a cut—more than one cut—above the makers of the rims in the baths. He handed the receiver to her. As she took it and passed him to get to the mouthpiece, he blurted . . .

"You don't happen to have a spare egg?"

"What?"

"Nothing. Go on with your call, I'll wait".

She looked nonplussed, not taking her eyes off him until he had retreated to the far end of the passage and turned to look out of the window. She talked briefly and he heard the receiver click back. He turned. She was on the way to her door, was opening it . . . She paused, seeing that he was approaching.

"You said something".

"Yes. I . . . er . . . An egg. Only if you have one to spare . . ."

"I think I have. Come in".

He followed her into the room and was struck at once by the contrast to his. It was clean, newly painted and curtained . . .

"I say".

"What?"

"What a nice room! It's the same as mine, I mean, but yours is nice. Are you sure?"

"Of what?"

"About the egg. I've been away for a few weeks and I don't have anything in".

"What are you going to eat with the egg?"

"I have a couple of biscuits".

She smiled and he saw how very attractive she was. She went to her folding kitchen store and it worked, the hinges oiled after painting, the shelves prettied with paper, fringed with gingham. Everything—like Miss Walker—was clean, orderly and kind looking. She produced a large plate and put on to it half a small loaf, a lump of butter, two rashers of bacon, a tomato . . .

"I say, I don't want all that . . ."

"No?"

"Yes. As a matter of fact, it'd be super but what about you?"

"I stocked up. I have plenty".

She added a small pot of marmalade and handed the plate to him, putting two eggs on to it at the last moment.

"Don't break them".

"Not till I get them downstairs".

"And you'll need some milk . . ."

"No. Yes. Thank you so much".

"Which floor are you on?"

"One below".

"Give me the eggs, I'll bring them. And the milk".

"No . . ."

"Don't keep saying 'No. Yes.'. I'm Imogen Walker, by the way".

"I'm Tighson. Christopher. The other way round, though".

Lack of sleep, over-indulgence, under-eating . . . Something made him only just make sense.

"Let's go, then".

He was reluctant to leave this little Dresden nest, that's how it looked to him. But not that fragile. Solid, unassailable Dresden, near unbreakable.

They walked down to his door and Christopher said . . .

"Don't come in!"

"Thank you!"

That smile appeared, and the crinkles that went with it.

108

One corner of her mouth tilted higher than the other when she smiled.

"That must have sounded awful. But . . . after your room . . . It looks so perfect and mine is as much a mess as I am . . . Come in!"

She broke into laughter that had a dozen delectable notes in it and he opened the door for her. She made straight for the culinary section.

"What's this?"

"It was coffee".

She poured it into the sink and there was a clunk as the solid lump hit the rim of the outlet.

"What's that?"

"I say again, coffee. It didn't even melt in boiling water, that's interesting . . ."

"And undrinkable" she said.

She picked up the lump—with beautifully manicured finger and thumb—and put it into the bin. Within moments, she was boiling a kettle, cooking eggs and bacon and toasting two pieces of bread. Christopher was laying a small table from his limited cutlery supply.

"Please, you don't have to do all that" he said.

"You left it a bit late before you said it. Don't you want me to? No, yes. Don't be silly, it's fun. Will you watch the eggs while I go up and get some coffee? Do you take sugar?"

"But . . . Miss Walker . . ."

"Or would you rather have just hot milk?"

"Yes. No".

They both laughed more than it warranted, and she left. Neither had made—nor had wanted to make, he was sure he thought for her too—the ghost of a pass. Each, he felt, acknowledged the personability of the other, even the attraction. But if they were drawn, they were not pulled. They were enjoying each other in a way that was neither animal nor devoid of animality. Whatever the time ahead might hold, it would not be ticked away by hurry. There was health in the mucky air. And Dresden clearness. For absolutely no reason he could think of afterwards, Christopher said aloud . . . "Back to normal".

109

14

"Dorking" said Dorian Gray.

"Yes, it is, isn't it?"

Gray laughed—one or two notes, none of them delectable. And no crinkles. No wrinkles either, had they been lifted away? Or hadn't he lived? Christopher dived—rudely, he was sure—back to reading.

"I brought a Sunday paper in case you want to see one".

"Thank you. Miss Walker, you're terribly sweet. You're the nicest thing that has happened to this dreadful building in the just over a year I've been here".

"Oh?"

"Yes. And no 'No'."

"Why is it dreadful?"

"Only two bathrooms and a caretaker who'd be good casting for Madame Lafarge. And not a lick of paint since I can't imagine when. Except for your room. You had to do that yourself, at an easy guess?"

"Yes. I'm studying interior design, it was good practice".

"Judging by results, you're going to be an instant success. I wish they'd get you to do over the whole place".

"They may".

"Oh?"

"Here's your breakfast" she said, hurriedly, and served it to him.

"I take it you've had yours?"

"Yes".

"Miss Walker. May I offer you some coffee?"

"Mr. Tighson . . . Yes".

They sat, and he ate with enormous appetite, she drinking a little coffee. He told her—asked by her to do so—about himself, about the play, about his hopes for the future. She was thrilled to hear that he was an actor, she hoped, one day, to design for the theatre. He had written a play, too? Might she read it?

"I'm rewriting completely. Paul Bannerman advised me to" he said, to impress. Then back to normality . . . "He was kind enough to read it and thinks it's awful. He's right, it is".

"There's a piece about him in the paper . . ."

"Today's? About Paul?"

"They're telling the full story about that girl who committed suicide".

"May I see?"

He took up the newspaper, knocking his knife on to the floor. SUSAN CHASE—THE STORY THEY NEVER TOLD he read. There was her picture and one of Paul beside it. A brief mention of the new play, about to open in London, provided the brand new spade for digging . . .

"May I . . . keep this?"

"There's something in it I want to cut out, I'll give it to you later".

"Thank you. Thank you".

He put the paper aside, took a clean knife from a drawer —not to offend—and finished off his meal.

It was half an hour before he could, decently, despatch Miss Walker. He devoured the Sunday article like a second breakfast. It was the first of a series of three—perfect timing, the third would appear on the Sunday preceding their London opening. Publicity. Good, bad? Hurtful, it was certain, to Paul. But not to the play, you couldn't offer a greater attraction to the public than, say, a leading man stabbing his leading lady. No, that wouldn't do, he'd be in jail. But lives laid bare, as bodies by a surgeon's knife, could draw to the box-office in a way that no kind, happy

111

occasion could. Death was news. Life, journalistically, was death.

It was a disjointed tale. The more Christopher read, the truer seemed to be Basil's remembered words "Nobody knew her . . .". The 'full story' was less than half empty. Susan Chase, wonderful actress, poor upbringing—posing for photographers . . . 'NUDE PICTURES NEXT WEEK . . .' He wondered what agony Paul would suffer at this dredge-up from the bottom of a pool he had thought to be still. An affair with an older man, Karl Engel . . . her one night London success and her darting away, like a selective moth, to brighter light. Engel's suicide soon after their arrival in California . . . All this was outlined, in brief, above and the first part of the story began with her childhood . . .

All he had had was breakfast but the rubbish bin was full to the brim.

Basil telephoned next morning early and Imogen Walker knocked on Christopher's door.

"It's for you".

"For me? Nobody ever rings me".

"Somebody has".

"Thank you so much. Here's your paper, by the way . . ."

"I'll put it under your door later".

Basil was apologetic. "Didn't quite know whether you'd be there, old son . . ."

"I've been here all the time".

"Oh. Oh? Oh. Well. What I telephoned for was . . . are you taking the train? That's a bloody silly question, of course you are . . . But what I mean is do you want to?"

"No. Why?"

"Care for a lift?"

"Not half".

"Give me your address and I'll pick you up after lunch. You are having lunch?"

"I think so".

"Eating is a thing you have to be certain about. Do it here, why don't you?"

"Er . . ."

"Cecily's got something on the hob. Delighted to have you share . . . Never mind all that, just be here at twelve-thirty—suit?"

"Suit. Thank you so . . ."

He'd rung off.

"See the Sunday papers?" Basil asked as they passed Gerrard's Cross.

"Only one".

"*The* one?"

"You mean . . . ?"

"Paul is terribly upset" said Cecily.

She sat behind Basil, Christopher in the front seat. Looking back, at her remark, he could admire the set of the head on her shoulders, she had tremendous style, this woman. The pallid beauty of the face and the long, smooth neck. The red of the hair—startlingly more alive than the deeper red of Imogen Walker's.

"You've spoken to him?" he asked.

"He telephoned last night" Basil said.

"Basil and I were through it with him, you see" Cecily added. "All of it".

"And it means . . . that much? Still?"

"Poor bugger doesn't get a chance to find out" said Basil. "Like taking a knock-out pill and then having someone shake you every five minutes. How can you tell whether you might or might not sleep it off? You can't blame the Press. Blame anyone, blame the public. Blame us. I confess I look forward to seeing a picture of S. Chase starkers . . ."

"Basil!"

"Nothing but the truth from me, old girl. Not many husbands could say that to their wives. And, if I didn't know the story, I'd probably lap it up the next two Sundays with the worst of 'em. We're a sorry lot, people. Stop for tea?"

113

Oxford was something of a bore for everyone but Christopher who renewed the odd acquaintance. People seemed to walk eight abreast on the narrow pavements and if you stepped into the road you could be killed by a bicycle. The theatre he found to be atmosphereless, the stage too wide. And the notice in the Isis was appalling—to Christopher, already, they were fourth form clever. They patronised him personally but damned the play out of hand as being 'entertainment'. A dirty word? The stars—who had spent a lifetime in leading up to brilliance in portrayed spontaneity—were dismissed as 'playing themselves'. The commercial newspapers were sycophantic and over praising. At least, the Isis flowed . . .

Liane wasn't speaking to him, Jackie didn't write.

Even as they left the stage after the second performance on the Saturday, St. Tropez was being torn to calculated pieces. Christopher came down to collect a jacket for Basil —he had to leave this on the set during the action and the A.S.M. had neglected to bring it to his room—and caught them fully at it. He was amazed at the speed of the work. The overtime pay meant less to the stage hands than the hurry home for the week-end. They all had well paid jobs during the day and made, in all, what would seem like a fortune to Christopher. If they were ill, they got sick pay— actors never do. If they struck, they drew strike pay. British Equity has no fund for this. If they were bone idle and could produce enough children they could earn more than in any of the other circumstances . . .

"What concerns me, old Chris, is their feet".

"Feet?"

"During the play. Time was, they wore plimsolls, couldn't hear a sound from 'em. Now, from the noise they create offstage when you're trying to create a laugh on, they wear Army boots. Their tongues are as loose as their feet are heavy. I know an actor who left the stage in tears after a Hamlet soliloquy. And the tears had nothing to do with his reluctance to kill his step-father. They were because his best had been forced into his worst by the intrusion of offstage tramp and talk".

"Couldn't they be sacked?"

"Of course. But not replaced. Thereby hangs the ever more drooping tail of the world . . . Ever see them put their filthy mits on the flats when they strike? Strike the scenery, I mean?"

Their care for the preservation of the canvas—so carefully painted—was nil, he now saw. The stage manager watched anxiously in case it should be marked or torn but his 'control' of the hands had to be tactful to a ludicrous point. If they struck . . .

The stage management would work into the morning to achieve the 'get-out', over tip the hands and see the bruised scenery on its way to Brighton. Next week, St. Tropez would be followed here by another venue in wood and canvas. If it chanced to be a 'low life' setting, would the hands handle with more care, he wondered . . . Christopher got the hell out and up the stairs.

They arrived ahead of the rest of the cast, giving a lift to the 'walking' understudy who covered the male star and Basil. A rather nebulous character who would certainly never play. The star and Basil belonged to a school that didn't believe in standing down. Short of being laid off by cholera.

Sookie's house stood at the far end of a quarter of a mile of drive. Christopher couldn't see it clearly but he didn't care for the silhouette. Basil manoeuvered his six year old Packard about among some dozen of vehicles, coming to rest at last between a Rolls and a Jensen.

'Slumming" he said to his car, giving the dashboard a pat in apology as he switched off.

A butler opened the door and Sookie appeared—the prescribed number of feet behind him and at the prescribed moment. Christopher didn't know who did the prescribing. But he did have inner promptings that were above his born station. He didn't think Sookie should have worn a black tie, for instance. The lilac smoking-jacket spoke casually—if loudly—but the other items of formal attire disagreed. A few strangers could be seen in dinner clothes. Nothing had been said about this on the invitation, Also, the formal guests—and their host—had already eaten. They would attend now at the spectacle of a company of under dressed actors, tucking in, hungrily . . . Sookie did nothing without purpose. Would the effect be that actors are, after all, rogues and vagabonds? Managers, pretenders to breeding?

Basil read his thought. "Gives 'em an edge . . ." he said, not lowering his voice.

Basil held the theory that people tended not to hear things they were not expecting to hear. He had proved this, to Christopher's amazed satisfaction, during the Newcastle week by shouting "Fuck" at the top of his voice in Woolworth's.

They stood before the loaded board now, and Cecily was helping them both to mixed plates.

"The one thing managers can't forgive, of course, is the fact that, whereas—at a boring and often, financially speaking, unsuccessful push—we don't need them, they do need us. By and large, they're a collection of megalomaniac nuts. Frustrated playwrights, actors, directors . . . folk frustrated in the simpler art of human intercommunication. People manqués. They talk with their cheque books. It's a language that, I suspect, bores the arse off them. It does me".

Cecily gave him a plate of food and a look to go with it. White jacketed Adonises drifted about, carrying trays of glasses. Only champagne. Christopher collected three.

"You could have his bum for the asking" said Basil as the white coat passed. Cecily turned with a plate of food for Christopher.

"Will you, for Christ's sake, shut up!" she said.

She handed Christopher his plate, giving his arm a squeeze as though to say no reflection on him. Then she forced a cold way past Basil and went to greet the older female star of *Lady in the Sun* who had just made her entrance.

"Blow me down" Basil said.

"Is Cecily all right?"

116

"Not like her to go off like that. Not the first time though, these last weeks. Must wheel her in for servicing when we hit the metropolis . . ." He continued to look in her direction. "What was I saying?"

"Perhaps . . ."

"Don't you start! What I mean is, really . . ." he went on, holding his plate in his right hand and working at the food with his left . . . "How the bloody hell people can be expected to break up lettuce with a fork . . . What I mean is we're all a rum lot—actors, managers, directors, even playwrights . . . Creators, by and large—leaving out the managers, of course . . . I suspect old God is a rum bird . . . Well, all that 'Three in one' for a start . . . But we're never more pathetic than when we step out of our proscenium . . ."

"How do you mean?"

"Ever play polo?"

"No . . ."

"Sookie doesn't aspire to it yet, I don't think his bum could stand the extra wear and tear. But it's becoming a great cult with actors. Not a sport, as it is with the aristos, but a cult. They play the gentleman from time to time on stage and, having tasted blue blood, they get the fancy to play him offstage too. It isn't quite an analogy but there was a fellow in New York . . . about the time I went there in *Galatea* . . ."

"You were in *Galatea*?"

"Now, this was a . . . What?"

"I'm sorry. I've been trying to buy a copy all week, it's on my mind. I didn't know you were in it . . ."

"Of course I was in it, they got me for peanuts. If you'd said I'd have lent you mine. Now that you have, I will still. Still will. What a bloody silly language! Where was I?"

"This fellow in New York . . ."

"Yes. As I say, it isn't an analogy at all. This fellow, this actor . . . played a lawyer on the wireless for so many years, five times a week, he took to dressing like a lawyer, joined a lawyers' club and used to give out advice on legal matters to all who wanted it and to many who didn't. He

117

ended up in a looney bin. Where's the Good Fairy with the champers . . . Ah!"

They received a glass each and Christopher, looking away to avoid the spaniel eyes, caught a sight of Liane sharing an armchair with Pauline. They were managing to sit face to face on it.

"Having a têton à têton" Basil said. His mouth closed on a fork-full of something very expensive but not identifiable. He expressed both adjectives with a facial mobility that made Christopher laugh aloud.

"That's what I mean" said Basil. "We can't stop acting. Where was I?"

"Actors playing polo".

"Yes. Playing gentlemen playing polo. They meet the real stuff chukkah by jowl and the Five and Nine doesn't half show. All down for the accolade in Act Three. Of course, you don't use it . . ."

"Use what?"

"Leichner's Five and Nine. The young go in for all this new crap . . ."

"Allow me to tell you, sir, I wouldn't be without it. Five and Nine . . . and a bit of Eight . . . You taught us".

"I did? I use Max Factor Pancake . . ." He raised his glass. "Here's looking you up in *Who's Who* . . ."

They drank. All at once, they could smell scent and Sookie was saying . . .

"Basil . . . darling! Sing something for us? In your own time, of course . . . Want your opinion of my new Blüthner . . ."

15

The number of guests had increased to more than fifty. Christopher had pushed to the back of his mind the inevitability of the party's end. It was a huge joke dreamed up by Basil and shared by the rest of the play company? His confidence had begun to return, a situation helped by the fact that he was now at alcoholic ease. He wished he could waft a little of the feeling to Cecily who, pale and silent in a far corner, appeared to be listening attentively to three stars, talking at once, who were oblivious of her.

"Quite a gathering" Basil said. "Not usually this many to attend a raping".

"Oh, shut up!" Christopher came back at once. Then he blushed to the roots and said "I'm terribly sorry".

"Don't be, old lad. Everybody's telling me to shut up tonight. You're not the only victim of the system, you know. Old Paul will be shitting himself. He won't turn up here, that's for certain. He goes on the rack for the second time tomorrow. Butchered to make a British Sunday . . ."

He took a glass neatly from a nearby, drifting tray and downed half the contents in one. Then he put an arm round Christopher's shoulders, looked around him and acted the expansive cosmopolitan.

"Now, whom don't you know?" he asked. "I mean by sight. As I said—or did I?—the dinner jackets are mostly managers. And the odd angel. Oh, and there's a critic. Of that I disapprove. I don't think the minced meat should be compelled to hob-nob socially with the mincer, do you? Ah, sad . . ."

119

Christopher followed his look to a far corner—near to Cecily whose colour had returned . . .

"Fellow with the worried look is one of the few managers who know half their onions. He has a play on called *Cloth of Gold* . . ."

"Super. I saw it".

"It's starless, mortgaged to the hilt and guesting in a Neil Lamont theatre. Reason for the worried look is he doesn't know whether Sookie is going to foreclose . . ."

"Jackie said something . . ."

"Worried Look has a trump card. He has Royals coming in next week and it will bump up the business, he'll be certain of a transfer. I don't think he'll need it. Sookie is mad about Royals, I don't know a manager who isn't. They all of 'em, to a near man, have the walls of their offices covered with framed enlargements of Royals shaking them by the hand—the thoughts of the Royals are not recorded in 'think' balloons. It's one thing managers and actors have in common. They'd accept a permanent physical bent forward condition for one light tap on the shoulder with that sword. Managers buy it with money. Literally, if a venal Prime Minister needs helping out, or by putting on prestige plays that lose it—to me, that's buying with money. Actors buy it with the proceeds of a sale of dignity. Or a more complete sell-out of themselves. Take little Jamie over there . . ." He indicated a famous, stunted actor who had joined a group that included the male star of their play and St. John Pender. 'Jamie' was contriving to smile and talk at the same time. ". . . I give him full marks. He has a minimal talent and has achieved maximal success. Even produces his own films, good ones, he's an arch little picker of brains . . . Now, you must have heard about Jamie—he's slipping if you haven't. Hasn't got so much as a C.B.E. yet—even Sookie has that. But he's sweating out a knighthood so hard his laundry bill must be astronomical . . . Opening hospitals, closing slums . . . Cancer Research charity dos, Spastics—there isn't a single human distress he doesn't buzz around like a blue arsed fly over a shit heap. Does good, unquestionably. If that's the word.

120

In the profession, he's everybody's good Jamie. But how is it that we all *know*?"

Basil fingered his glass and peered at the liquid as though he couldn't understand how it came to be still there.

"There was an old poet . . ." he went on, addressing the wine—seemingly in final salute . . . ". . . who said 'Do good by stealth and . . . BLUSH . . ." (the wine shivered at the word) . . . ". . . to find it fame' . . . I like the force of that word 'blush' . . ."

He began to put the glass to his lips, then paused, adding —to Christopher . . .

"You'd be astonished at the number of actors whose wives are magistrates. From rogues and vagabonds to sinks of respectability in three uneasy generations . . ."

As he drank, he had another afterthought and spluttered in expressing it.

"Queers . . ." he said, and gave a slight belch . . . 'Queers will marry and even father a brat or two to give propriety to that eager, dipping shoulder. Over there, for instance . . ."

Christopher saw a dilapidated but still famous film star Knight. Even he had heard the appalling tale of the wife who had flown out to a far East film location to be with him, only to find him sharing a hotel suite with a young actor whom he had insisted on having with him in the cast. The wretched woman had returned to London by the next plane.

"What I don't understand is . . ." Christopher began . . .

"How it seems to be that everyone knows but the wife? I think she does know. It's either a mother wish or an over addiction to the sensitivity that women say makes a good lover . . . Or sheer arrogance, 'I'm the one to change him' . . . It's put more women on return planes.

As they helped themselves to trifle from a huge bowl a murmur of voices, begun in the acre of room beyond, grew until it surrounded them. They heard applause. And Sookie's voice from a long way off . . .

"Ladies and gentlemen . . . we are to be honoured by a song from Mr. Basil Smart . . ."—a hand held up to stave off reaction— ". . . if he can tear himself away from the

121

flesh pots . . . *and* from that gorgeous young man whose name escapes me for the moment but whose salary I have a feeling I'm paying . . ."

Through the laughter and clapping that followed the announcement, Basil said . . . "Here we go. Wish me luck, gorgeous. Cecily thinks I'm going to endanger our future. If our future depends upon smiling up the arses of such as Sookie, she may have a point. People should have more faith, though. Pissed, I may be. Anybody's fool, I am not . . ."

Amid a growing volume of applause, Basil made his way to the piano. He drew a laugh from his apparent inability to find it. Christopher followed him, at a slight distance, making for the corner in which Cecily sat, white faced now. He sat on the floor beside her and she took his hand as somebody lowered the lights. Basil was seated and peered at the assembly as though they were difficult to see . . .

"Who does the lighting here?" he asked. "The minute I'm on, everything goes down to half!"

A huge laugh greeted this and he let his fingers run over the keys. He reacted to the sound.

"It's a hun!" he said. "This piano is definitely a hun". Laughter. Christopher felt the grip tighten from Cecily.

"For a hun, sensitive, I will say that . . ." Laughter. "And a bass like the ring of bloody doom . . ." Laughter. And a cascade of notes, skilfully drawn from the beautiful instrument. Basil would have given a lot to own it. With perfect timing, he allowed his audience to murmur appreciation. Then, still playing . . .

"A little song I penned myself, though I say it as should . . . Only one song, that's all you're getting . . . I'm not the only goose for cooking tonight . . ."

He played the line straight at Sookie who roared with delight and shot a look at Christopher. Through the general laughter, Christopher took his hand away from Cecily's and wiped it with a discreet handkerchief. She took it again. Basil was singing . . .

Oh to be a social, social stage star
Terribly, terribly, terribly in the swim . . .
You would never catch me acting,

122

It's degrading and exacting,
I'd spend my time in climbin', climbin' out on a ducal
limb . . .
Oh to crash the gate of the Royal Enclosure,
To rub the noblest elbows in the land . . .
I'd fiche myself, I fear,
Of being the actor of the year
If Douglas Fairbanks shook me by the hand . . .

The assembly gave him laughter. Timing his re-entry to perfection, Basil went on . . .

Oh to be a social, social stage star,
Terribly, terribly, terribly in the news . . .
Not so much for playing Othello
As for being the sort of fellow
Who touches Royal Duchesses and Colonels in the
Blues . . .
Oh to spend a holiday on a grouse moor
With influential Cabinet M.P.s . . .
You'd always catch me bending
In case an accolade was pending,
I'd get lots and lots of practice on my knees . . .

The melody, such as it was, was bouncey and a touch old-fashioned but suited the song and the piano style. More and louder laughter. Basil seemed to assume the exception of present company and present company, where the caps fitted, grateful for the assumption, was with him all the way . . .

Oh to be a social, social stage star,
Terribly, terribly forward in the queue . . .
Over tailored, over witty,
And on every ball committee,
I'd give pounds and pounds to charity instead of the
revenue . . .
Oh to be goin' a-huntin' with the Pytchley . . .
A jump ahead of the fox I'd always be . . .
When the honours at last they divvied
I'd be absolutely livid
If I finally got the M.B.E.—
I would return it
If I only got the M.B.E.!

A flourish at the keyboard and a thunder of reception from his audience, Jamie leading it. Basil left the piano, miming exhaustion after great effort, and came to join Cecily and Christopher. The surrounders congratulated him . . .

"When did you dream that one up, eh?"

"Meant every word" said Basil to a dozen half listeners. "Tragedy of being a clown . . . Nobody believes . . ." Strictly for the ears of his wife and Christopher, he added "Bit of luck, really . . ."

Cecily looked up at him, no more chiding in her eyes, just adoration.

"The peak of a theatrical social occasion," said Basil, "is when the certainty is established that nobody—but absolutely *nobody*—is listening to anybody else. Like about now . . ."

The noise was deafening and the talk had the shrillness of unreality.

"Nobody like us for projecting the old voice" he added.

Christopher looked about him. "Surely all these people aren't staying?" he asked.

"Have to sleep in the garden if they are. Not that this place couldn't billet a couple of platoons. Back to London, mostly".

"Long drive".

"Not too long. An invitation from Sookie is a Royal Command. Some of them will go back to Oxford, put up there".

"So it'll be just the company?"

"Staying? Plus a bumble of queers. Thank you, yes".

Basil took yet another glass of champagne. "This stuff flows like the Isis. The river, not the magazine", he said.

"I don't think it would approve, do you? The magazine, not the river".

"Now, that's where you're wrong, old Chris. If that bloody left-wing critic were here tonight he'd be under the Blüthner by now. There are no readier partakers of goodies than those who decry the partakers. Like the staunch Red politicians who live, secretly, for the day when they will move up to the Lords. You're not worried, are you? About later?"

"Not too much. I wish I had you to write my dialogue".

There were no parlour games. A long haired, nervous and no longer very young man sat at the piano and played floridly, hitting what Basil called 'fistfuls' of wrong notes. A few couples danced. Christopher got the impression that even the most obviously heterosexual among the men were hesitant about displaying their normality. The dancing was half hearted, the women, too, not wanting to offend? It was his first experience of a social event in which the non-virile pretended virility and embarrassed the virile into no pretence at all. Natural behaviour contracted itself into a self-conscious tight rope walk.

It occurred to Christopher that nearly everyone present needed to get into or remain in Neil Lamont's good books. It occurred to him, too, to wonder whether this was what theatre was about. Was it not possible to learn your job and do it well and be acclaimed for it?

The heteros were deeply in the minority. And, as the time wore on, the odds on the odds became shortened, the heteros being the first to leave. He looked about him and felt like a subaltern in a forward, exposed position with only one platoon who were now deserting by the dozen. Basil had taken Cecily to bed and had whispered that he thought he'd turn in too.

"Driving to London tomorrow after lunch . . ."

"May I come with you?"

"Of course. Good luck. Remember it's a great life if you weaken . . ."

"Not me".

"See you, then . . ."

In a moment of decision, he grabbed Liane's understudy and began dancing. Something about this atmosphere that made you overdo the hetero bit. If you weren't careful. Careful? Why the bloody hell should you be careful not to show that you are a natural born ram and proud of it?

He crushed the understudy to him and she gave out a noise like a sat on air cushion with a leak.

"Sorry" he said.

"That's . . . all right . . ." she answered and gazed up at him. The things people misunderstand . . .

Briefly, he caught the eye of Sookie. It seemed to approve the height, the width. The virility . . . Panic made Christopher dance with more vigour. Then he wondered if he should be doing that, show that you're a man and put him off? It might put him on! Sookie would surely be the female half of any proposed relationship? He danced more slowly.

"Oh, Christ" he said, under his breath.

"Pardon?" said the understudy, continuing to gaze . . .

The car doors were still banging, over-voiced goodbyes still being bleated into the night air.

Christopher stood a little away from and studying the group that remained. All members of the cast of *Lady in the Sun*. Suddenly he felt a swelling pride in them. The three stars who had spent so much time in the theatre, two of them acquiring such skill, exhibiting it. He was tempted to applaud them now, as so many hundreds of thousands had applauded over the years. The male star was perhaps the top man in his field. Ageing a little, he wore a toupee even off stage, cleverly made, meticulously applied—Christopher thought what a chore it must be to do all that and shaving too. Daily. It was magnificently in place still. Though its wearer had overdrunk and swayed just noticeably as he stood. The female star—the talented one—squeezing his arm as though to say "Sookie won't mind, darling. He knows you don't drink in the theatre . . ." The respect these two had, one for the other. Christopher knew that he did. Drink in the theatre, from a growing fear. Will the magic be there tomorrow night? Will the lines be there? He looked pathetic now, as he waited to say his goodnights. Christopher loved them all. Even the female star with not so much talent had a presence, had proved a need for her. A 'personality' they said she was, well . . . better that than an actress who

126

acted hard and badly, she knew her limitations. Yes, he loved her too. And the others of the group, the smaller part actors, the understudies. Even Liane . . . To see them like worried children, waiting for a pat on the head from a tyrant father . . . that stinking poof who knew from nothing but money bags and couldn't father the miscarriage of a Yorkshire terrier if you fed him male hormones for a year . . .

Christopher took a half full glass of champagne from a nearby table and raised it—he was far from being sober himself, he realised—to the male star.

"To you, sir . . . and please forgive me . . . for . . ."

The male star beamed a warm smile at him. His companion, taking her cue, smiled too.

"You're all right, young 'un . . ."

"Yes" said his companion.

Liane hugged Pauline a little tighter and smiled too.

We're all on a bloody raft, thought Christopher. We made it ourselves and it's all we have and the sea can't be relied upon to be friendly . . . As he was about to drink . . .

"Darlings . . ." said Sookie, who had popped up out of the waves with shark teeth and wasn't on anybody's side . . . 'Drinkies before bye-byes?"

"No" they said, knowing he didn't mean it, and the unreal chatter began as they moved to the door . . .

"Don't go, Christopher . . ."

They sat side by side—Neil Lamont at his left—on a sofa with wall ends held up by heavy silken cords, tasselled. Christopher tried hard to recall the script Basil had used but his mind was a wine blank. Sookie lisped a speech at him made up of flattery and cosy concern. As he paused to take a breath—opening his mouth wide, with a sickening smack of the lips—Christopher came in with . . .

"Do you think the play will run, sir?"

"Well, now . . . Do you speak unselfishly, have you the welfare of the play at heart, my welfare, the welfare of your fellow actors . . . and actresses . . . ? Or are you thinking about your own future?"

Bastard.

"Both, sir. I mean, all of them. Sir".

"Couldn't you be persuaded to drop the 'sir'?"

Like a hot cake, he could.

"I . . . wouldn't feel quite right . . ."

"I'm 'Sookie' to my friends. Are you one?"

Christopher knew that close association with Basil had pushed his face into a Basil expression. Sookie laughed.

"One of my friends, I meant" he said . . . and Christopher laughed in return. Play it for comedy, this was the way.

"I hope so, sir . . . I mean . . ."

" 'Sookie' ".

"Sookie".

"That's better. Doesn't it feel better?"

"Er . . ."

Sookie had patted his knee with a warm hand and had omitted to withdraw it.

"Yes. Yes, it does".

Christopher had spoken as a reflex. He looked down at the hand and back to Sookie and saw that he had mistaken the line of dialogue. Basil, for Gawd's sake. How does it run? The hand began to slide upwards on his thigh and Christopher looked at it, unable to speak or move. One quick witticism now, or was it already too late? Something far back in his brain, some ancient control, governed his tongue, held him motionless. At once, he knew what it was. A yearning to be certain. And he hoped to God there wouldn't be that many opportunities hereafter . . . He relaxed, consciously, let the hand continue its journey. It found its mark after a moment and began the caressing. That damned tell tale hardening, it would sicken him now to vomiting if it should happen. It had been Sookie's right hand and now it was his left, the right hand and arm about his shoulders, the left caressing, working at him. No reaction. He discounted the mounting nausea, there was no automatic physical response, no blood pumping into his gland . . . If he gave a whoop of joy now would the creature on his left mistake that too?

It was the smile of relief on his face that Sookie mistook. Suddenly, he was on his knees before the boy, look-

128

ing up at him, suppliant, caressing with both hands, fumbling at buttons . . . Incredulity, horror, paralysis. Then Christopher crashed through this and rose clumsily to his feet, sending Sookie reeling to the floor.

"I'm . . . I'm sorry . . . sir . . ." he said.

His back was to Sookie, he couldn't turn at once, had to lessen the triumph. When he did turn, Sookie was on his feet, smiling down at the cigarette he pressed into a holder. Christopher went on . . .

"I'm . . . not like that, you see, I . . . like girls . . ."

The lighter obeyed Sookie and he lit the cigarette, drew on it and released the smoke. Slowly, he brought his look up to Christopher.

"You poor, dear boy . . ." he said, with complete composure . . . ". . . Never mind".

After a muttered "Goodnight", Christopher left the room, hugging his new-found certainty to him like a trophy won. His loss he was not able to assess.

16

The smile of remembered triumph still on his face, Christopher looked up and saw D. Gray. Esquire . . . Deep, or appearing to be deep, in an expensive looking book. Triumph. The chin of triumph dips down, draws back in the presence of pathos. You couldn't think of D. Gray as anything but pathetic. Or could you? Do they lack something or do they have something more than you have? Are they enviable? No, not that, Christopher decided. Do they envy *you*, do they find *you* pathetic? What do they think of the man of the seventies, with hair that hides his potential war serviceability, puts him among the women? Does the hair turn them off? Or on? Did they think of them as women in the first place and did the hair help? It depended, Christopher supposed, on where they stood—or didn't—in the framework of kink. If they liked to be done—as Sookie, he was sure, did—they would want you to be manly. Hair, yes. All over you, perhaps! If you were a 'doer'—as he supposed D. Gray might be—you would like your minion . . . how? Long haired, looking like a woman? Or skinhead, or boy who is, surprisingly, woman, or not even that but broken into it? Like a busted bronco? And did the 'doer' derive a bonus pleasure from the breaking or would he be just as happy doing a queer who liked to be done? Christopher's mental vision was filled with a view —in Cinemascope—of D. Gray astride N. Lamont, riding him like a bronco, beating that brown curly brimmed bowler up and down the impressario's flanks.

He could not but feel that they had more than their share of joy in new conquest. In perverting, in fact. And the more difficult they found it to twist healthy beings into unhealthy, the greater the excitement. As in his, Christopher's, breaking new female ground at each bedding? No. It wasn't an analogy. He remembered a gasped phrase that had come from his mouth once, when in mid-deflowering . . .

"I'm not changing you into something you're not, I'm changing you into something you are . . ."

'Dear Gorgeous', the note ran . . . 'Cecily said to say sorry too, I left early—I think it best to get her home. At least two other cars going London-wards or Sookie will arrange for a car to take you to Oxford, trains not too bad. Forgive, but not avoidable. Hope you got your laughs . . . Till Bournemouth, Basil'.

It was delivered by a willowy catamite who, clearly, never could be called upon to play the husband, why did Sookie employ him? To add virility to himself by comparison, confuse issues? The catamite waited . . .

"Does Mr. . . . Is there . . . a car? I have to get to Oxford?"

"There's a bus from the main road".

"A bus . . . ?"

"It leaves at twenty minutes past the hour".

"Isn't there . . . ? Is nobody else in the party going to London?"

"After luncheon, there'll be several cars leaving . . ."

"I . . . don't think I . . . I have to get back. Thank you".

"Not at all".

The catamite smiled a knowing—or a guessing?—smile and slid away.

Christopher dressed quickly and began his journey through the vast, deserted house to the front door. He was grateful at this moment that actors are late risers. Not even a catamite to clutter the way. The clean, outside air was cold and made him shudder. The heavy door closed behind him, solid, unshaking. Final. Within a few paces stood the Rolls Royce which, he knew, belonged to Neil Lamont. Its back was towards him. Christopher loved luxury—on the merest acquaintance he was quite decided. It is hard to say goodbye, however temporarily, to so lush an object of the affections.

He began to walk.

On the train—late, unheated, dirty—Christopher shared with a million or so other readers of the newspaper the continuing intimate secrets in the life of Susan Chase. She was sprawled, in photograph too, naked across the page. The exposure was the more indecent for the fact that she had been a child of fifteen at the time. ESCAPE FROM FOSTER PARENTS, EARLY WORK AS A MODEL . . . The tiny breasts, the nothing of a waist, the faintness of pubic hair. Her hands—the fingers were pointed like the petals of flowers—half covered her face in shame or simulation of shame. The photographer had done well. 'Revelation' he had called it.

Christopher sat back and reflected that—quite inexplicably—he had objected, in mind, to the theatrical exposure —lesser exposure, surely—of nympho Jackie. If a man were deeply in love . . . He looked back at the picture, devouring it mentally as would the million or so. Sweet human nature, he thought. But continued to look.

The scaffolding didn't help. Cornwall Place had been at one time, Christopher supposed, a super place to live. If you were Victorian and believed in the Empire and the Englishman. And had money. You fathered a huge family, kept a staff of servants in the attic, your word was law. And your mistress never raised her pretty head at the wrong moment, order, all was order. With the crumbling of Empire, Cornwall Place should have crumbled too. But it was built too well. The Englishman had crumbled, in loyalty, but the anachronism of Cornwall Place remained. A falling bomb—helped perhaps by falling pieces of our own anti-aircraft shells—had ripped a bit off a cornice and had pitted the wall at one side. Repairs had never been made to these items of damage. The house wore them like medals. Right and proper.

"What the . . ." said Christopher as he peered through the tubular steel criss-cross to make sure that this was, indeed, Number Eleven. No workmen, of course, since this was Sunday. The Lord rested the seventh day and the British workman, God-like, rested too. Christopher always felt this to be something of a presumption. God did quite a stint in the six days preceding. Dare to be a Daniel.

He took the stairs four at a time. On the landing before his door he paused. The house, even the interior, had the air of no business-as-usual. Quiet, deathly quiet. And brick dust, cement, whatever it was, hung in the air. He unlocked his door and went in.

The contrast with his arrival just a week ago could be divided into two parts. Firstly, his room, as he saw it ahead of him through the open door, had been dusted and Ewbanked and looked like a cared for room. There were flowers in a vase. To his right though, instead of a fourth wall, there was sacking that hung from ceiling to floor to cover a gaping hole in the brickwork.

"God Almighty" he said.

As if in answer—albeit a female A.S.M. reading in for the

132

principal—came the voice from behind him, from his own doorway, lately entered . . . "Christopher . . ."

"Miss . . . Imogen . . ."

"Are you absolutely furious?"

"Is it the I.R.A.?"

She laughed, dutifully he felt. She was a jolly sweet Imogen. Wearing a housecoat with flowers all over it—the same flowers as stood in the vase!—and neat as a new made pin. Her red hair scraped back tight over the ears, lifted. Edwardian. Christopher liked it, it suited her. The waist was minimal. He thought of the naked waist of little, revealed Susan. For no reason.

"No, but are you? Furious? I somehow got the idea you wouldn't be back for a fortnight. That you'd go on to Bournemouth".

"There was a thought about driving straight there from Oxford. It was a wishful thought. Not that I didn't want to come back here . . . It's just . . ."

"Just that is isn't much like home? It will be. If you give me time . . ."

"You? Did you put those flowers there?"

"Yes. Did you mind?"

"Mind? They're very pretty. So are you . . ."

I've gone too far, he thought. This one isn't like the others.

"Thank you".

She didn't seem to be offended. She went on . . . "I also made the hole in the wall . . ."

"Oh" he said. "What were you doing, looking for something?"

She laughed again. "Would you like to come up to my room and I'll tell you all about it. Have you had tea?"

"I haven't even had lunch".

"Whenever we meet you've missed at least one meal . . . I'll make you something. That is if it's all right with you?" He looked into the clear green eyes, she was a refreshing change from all that had gone before. In the shape of last night. In the shape of all that had gone before, now that he came to admit it.

133

"So . . ." he said, pushing aside the plate that had held the cheese soufflé and which had taken the place of the plate that held the lamb cutlets and broccoli and jacket potato—following the mushroom soup, "your Daddy owns the building and he's giving you carte blanche about doing it over. I'm to have a kitchen that doesn't fold up and a bathroom all my own, no shillings needed, we all are . . ."

"There's only you and me. The others were given notice, it'll be all new tenants. I didn't tell you because I wanted to surprise you".

"With a hole in my wall?"

"It'll be beautiful when it's finished, just you wait".

She filled his glass again with claret as he considered the information she had fed him with the late lunch.

"You realise I shall have to leave? Like the others?"

"Leave? Why?"

"I'm paying for a room and a cupboard with pans in it. Paying for a room with kitchen and bathroom will be beyond the means of an actor about to open in London in his first play".

"It's a Bannerman play. It'll run".

"Of course. But if it didn't?"

"I wouldn't worry about that".

"But I do. Your Dad will have to put up the rents".

"It has nothing to do with Daddy".

"What?"

"He's given me the house. I can do as I like with it".

"Oh. Oh".

"That's twice you said 'Oh' ".

"I meant it both times. Am I permitted to ask who is paying for the alterations?"

"He is. I haven't any money of my own. I will have".

"From letting the rooms in this house?"

"Yes".

"Not much you won't. Not if you don't put up the rents".

"Of course I shall put up the rents. They'll be at least double".

"Which is where we came in and where I go out".

134

She began to clear the table. The green eyes looked back at him, fleetingly. "You're a special case" she said.

It was only after several moments that he was able to reply . . . "Oh".

There had, in fact, been an on-off arrangement about Bournemouth. They never, at any time, contemplated more than the Saturday night stay under Sookie's vast roof and Basil had said "Let's drive straight down after Sunday lunch". "I think that's silly" Cecily had said. "Let's take the car back to London and leave it. We'll go down on the Monday on the Bournemouth Belle".

"Won't it be nice to have the car?"

"In Bournemouth?"

"We could drive up one chine and down the next. Pop over to Studland, we could do that, I like Studland".

"We haven't been there for years".

"Then it's time we went again".

"You don't want to drive from Bournemouth back to London on the Saturday night after two shows".

"Who doesn't?"

"*I* don't. Want *you* to".

Basil and Christopher travelled down alone on the 'Belle'.

"The old girl didn't feel too good. Made her stay".

"Are you worried?"

"Sick, yes".

"Why didn't you stay with her? Sookie would understand, surely?"

"Of course he would. He'd put my understudy on for a week, we're played in, it wouldn't matter a damn".

"Then, why . . . ?"

"I need the pay packet".

"Don't they . . . if you . . . ?"

"Not even if it were me with a pain in my gut. 'No play, no pay', that's the rule—thought up by managers. Which is what gives rise to the brave saying 'The show must go on' —thought up by actors with a pain in their gut".

135

In the post rack at the theatre, there was a note from Jackie who had moved to Torquay . . . 'Good luck, you bastard'. He was dressing in her room too, he knew it right away. The scent lingered. A few balls of cotton wool in the drawers, some lipstick-covered—cleaners never were thorough. A reminder word, scrawled in greasepaint on the mirror . . . MASCARA . . .

As he unpacked his theatre bits and pieces and laid out his dressing-place Christopher wondered what made the difference between Jackie and Imogen. Theatre folk were brighter, quicker thinking, why? The need to armour your daily living with wit and thrust? Extravert meets extravert? Inhibitions? In the theatre they were ragged out of you, dragged out of you. You lost them but kept them filed. You wore a shell but it had to be readily detachable, you were a walking contradiction in terms. If you weren't vulnerable your acting wouldn't be worth a damn. But the click catches on the shell must be kept oiled, the shell itself highly polished. This demanded an alertness which was the brightened mind.

The stage doorkeeper thrust a script at him. "Mr. Smart said to give it", he said, economically. It was *Galatea.*

Christopher went straight to Basil's room. The understudy was there, trying on the Third Act jacket.

"Didn't you hear? Basil had to go back to London. I've been rehearsing since five".

"Nobody called me".

"I only have half a page with you. I've been going through the rest with the others—perhaps you'd be kind enough to run it while I make up?"

"Of course. But . . . Basil . . . Why . . . ?"

"His wife, somebody said. She's having an operation".

Christopher went back to the comfortable but lonely digs after the first night. He walked, thinking to get the sea air but could smell only petrol. He didn't care for the theatre—they all seemed to be designed by folk who were hell bent on wasting space. And who felt that the actors, being paid for their presence, should not be offered comfort into the bargain. The star dressing rooms were farthest from the stage, you couldn't find the lavatories. The stage had no rake, the auditorium itself . . . But then, he reflected, how did an architect gain experience in the design of theatres? They are not built often. The only hope would seem to be *not* to avoid a man who had made a mess of one theatre and give the job to a new man. The old mistake maker would do a better job, must, you would think. Imagine an actor making a balls of his first part and, therefore, not being cast again! The thought made Christopher shudder.

He was beginning to wish he'd taken a bus, these chine roads were confusing, at least he could have been dropped at the right starting point for the labyrinth . . .

The understudy had imitated palely and had 'failed to impress' was the phrase Christopher had seen used. The immense value to this play of Basil's performance. Of course, the cast congratulated the understudy, largely on knowing the lines, on getting through—was this admirable?

"Would you like to ring up?" the landlady asked. She was the first one, this tour, whose name he didn't know.

"Ring Mr. Smart? Oh no, I . . . I wouldn't want to . . . I don't know whether . . ."

"Don't let your meal get cold . . ."

With Basil's and Cecily's physical presences had departed the warmth, the cushion of 'family' he had come to lean upon. The cast had been happy, closely knit. Now . . . there was a mile of a breach.

Two nights later, Basil telephoned.

"The old lady's fine. Sends her love. She's sitting up in bed with tubes and things going in and out everywhere. Saline drip, I think is the word, and I'm on the mend too . . ."

"You?"

"I gave a blood transfusion. Just heroics. They've got gallons of the stuff and I had to insist on leaking all over them. Gives you a sort of nice feeling, after you've taken the tea and toast. I hope my blood's all right. It's the right

137

group I mean, but I wouldn't want to pass on my insanity to the girl I love. How goes the play? Don't tell me he gets that laugh in Act Two I never got?"

"No. He doesn't get any laugh in Act Two. Nor in Act One".

"Thank God. I'll be back tomorrow, by the way . . ."

"Tomorrow?"

"Nothing I can do here except hold the old hand. She's going to need a long, expensive convalescence. I'd better shoot back and get those laughs. She's going to miss our First Night . . ."

Wednesday of next week, Christopher thought with a jolt of horror.

"She'll have to catch us later" he said. "We'll be played in".

"Or played out".

"What do you mean?"

"Bit worrying, old Paul just telephoned. He's been to a first night in Chelsea somewhere. Says the play's going to set us all on our ears . . ."

"Oh?"

"New slant. Instead of building folk up, making 'em forget, you remind 'em. Tear 'em down".

"What play is it?"

"By a fellow nobody's ever heard of. Paul says we will, though. The play? Called . . . wait a minute . . . *Look Back . . . in Anger . . .*"

CHAPTER

17

What Christopher minded most was the break up of the family His love of comfort, his faith in a providing Fate . . . soon the faith would surely be shaken, comfort prove a whore. But the fellowship, the huddling close of shipmates before the vessel splits—when it does and the sea carries them off into four point night you'll never see them. Or, if you do, there will be a new permutation. A new family grouping, this one will never be repeated. Basil had warned him only last week . . .

"Strange thing, old soldier . . . First play I was in— *Galatea,* as I live and die. Did you get the script . . . ?

"Yes. But I haven't . . ."

"Went to New York. Great excitement and all that. I was the only original greenhorn, we had professionals there, the real job. Addresses we exchanged . . . Just like the package dealers on the Spanish beach . . . lifelong what'sit . . . sworn . . . I telephoned one lad when I got back to London and he talked to me as though I were a gipsy. Which, of course, I was. But so was he . . .

They were sitting in the Moulin d'Or in Romilly Street— Basil, Christopher and Imogen and, a late arrival, Paul Bannerman. George and Ernest, the proprietors, hovered unobtrusively, their mother sat at her desk. The real theatre loving runners of restaurants always know when to smile and frame success, when to be a background to sadness. Paul had ordered a steak and was waiting for it to grill.

"What's the verdict?" Basil asked, pouring a fourth cup of coffee for himself.

"We'll get that in the morning" Paul answered.

"You know what I mean. The little wake you just had with Sookie, what came of that?"

"He didn't care for the booing from the gallery".

"Nor did we. The bastards are organised, want to see it in the papers. The play went like a dream".

"Yes".

"Well, you can't deny it, it did!"

"The simile is perfect, Basil. You were all marvellous, I expected you would be. The play let you down".

"Balls" said Basil.

Christopher thought he saw Imogen flinch but he gave her no look of apology for his friend. He would have said it himself.

The play had had a good showing, every member of the small cast giving all they had. Giving too much? First

139

Nights can be occasions for too many stops being pulled too far out, now or never, this is for the critics. Not easy to keep an exact rein. But it had gone well. Then, at the third curtain call, the booing had come from on high. Angry stalls sitters had countered with shushing which sounded like hissing and they had stopped applauding meanwhile. Then renewed, loud—overloud—applause with louder booing, the fourth curtain call had been the last. The play's reception—through the evening—would have aroused expectation of a smash hit, ten curtains. Now . . .

"We'll have to wait" said Paul.

His steak was served by gentle, understanding hands and George moved swiftly away. Paul began to eat with no appetite. Christopher wondered how much weight had been added to his mental burden by the Susan Chase chapters —the last, three days ago, the most lurid and wounding. His work had engrossed him fully, his continuing success had pressed him urgently to work.

"You didn't answer my question" Basil said quietly. "Are we all going to be on the breadline? Some of us would like to know".

"Sookie is as bewildered as anybody. But you know Sookie, he goes with the tide. Whoever is pushing the tide at the moment doesn't like to hear laughter. If the theatre is going to be locked in gloom and social comment, I'm finished for one . . ."

"You think, overnight, audiences won't want to laugh?" asked Basil.

"They'll want to, you won't stop that, ever. Whether or not they'll be allowed to is up to Sookie and Co. and the pressures".

"Pressures?"

"Political? Who knows? They—whoever they are—are tired of seeing well dressed folk cavorting in expensive environments. The muffler, I suspect, will be 'in'. I can't write for the muffler".

"You could write social comment with the worst of 'em".

"I might be able to. But the kind of comment I would make wouldn't please pink ears. And I doubt if I could put

140

my heart into tearing down everything I love—which is the process about to be embarked upon".

"By the new writers? Who are they?"

"We don't know yet. The tumbrils have barely begun to rumble and the mass decapitation comes next. What comes after, who are to be the leaders, God alone knows. If they throw up a Shaw, it won't have been in vain. I suppose. But I've always been allergic to the sound of knives grinding".

There was a silence. Then Paul said . . .

"How's that Cecily?"

"Speaking of knives? She's pulling through. I telephoned her before the second act, she sent her love. I gave Chris his share, I hereby give you yours".

"You don't need to. I got a wire, she must have got the hospital to 'phone it through".

"So? I don't know that I approve of this wide dissemination of the affections. But I don't think she'll run out. I'm going to give her a slap-up time in Switzerland, did I mention it? On the proceeds from a smash called *Lady in the Sun*. That's what the old girl's going to be—Lady in the Mountain Sun . . . For three whole months . . ."

"If we don't hit?"

"Tell you one thing. I've never broken a promise yet. Not to that one. She'll be fast asleep by now, dreaming about it. I say, Imogen . . . Isn't she pretty, Paul? How did you come to take up with an actor? Christopher, apologise to the girl for all this shop talk. And some of the words you've been using, by Christ".

"Er . . ." Christopher began . . .

"I find it fascinating" Imogen interrupted. "And alarming, I happen to have enjoyed the play".

"Good" said Paul. "It was fairly historic, at least. You may well have been present at the demise of light comedy in our theatre".

"Nonsense," Imogen said. "I can't believe that a few booers can pass effective judgement".

"Talks well, doesn't she?" Basil said to Christopher. To Imogen, he said "It has happened, darling. More than a few times within the last year. Say something, old Chris".

141

"I'm just . . . numbed. I can't believe that Mr. Bannerman could be a back number . . ."

"He's back on the 'Mister Bannerman' kick" said Basil. Christopher ignored this and concluded . . . *"Lady in the Sun* is brilliant".

"Thank you" said Paul. "But it will be an offence to shine, don't you see? Rough up the shoes and the accent, take the loving crease out of the trousers. And don't wash. Then, mark my words, you will be on the way to joining the new, tear-down elite. Only, don't phrase it that way . . . Just say you're 'in'. I make another prophesy. In a short time 'star' will become a dirty word. The stars are the aristocracy of theatre and aristocrats will be freight in the tumbrils. 'They' will try to make their own stars, style will be something to be unlearned. They won't succeed, of course, but failure is what makes them tick and the booers at *Lady in the Sun* will be the clique that makes *Matey in the Mud* the play of the era".

He pushed his plate away, most of the food still on it. Then he said to Basil . . .

"Remember the first night of *Galatea*?"

"Do I not! Not a boo in those days".

"Remember old What-was-his-name . . . ?"

"Lord Dunham? He took us all to the Savoy Grill".

"Then down to Fleet Street to see the write-ups wet off the presses . . . Basil . . ."

"I can take it if you can. If we're making history I'd prefer not to get the lesson at breakfast. George, my bill! Ernest, any chance of a taxi? Chris, don't sit there looking as though you'd just been born, get the girl her coat . . ."

The reviews were uncannily alike. As though an overall directive had gone out from an authority higher than the Press Lords. The adjectives were shared, often, by critics of newspapers with widely differing policies. 'Flippant' was an obvious one, two 'insubstantials' not more than coincidence. But 'moribund'—and allied to the noun 'style' . . . Three times.

They were the most damaging columns Christopher had

142

ever read. Of a new play cast in the Bannerman mould. The last product of the mould was playing, still, to near capacity business at another theatre, nothing made sense . . .

They read them in corners, under street lamps, in the bald light from a coffee stall . . .

"It can't . . . It can't be . . ." said Basil. "Sookie won't be fool enough to take it off!"

"Have you ever known him to nurse a play? He's the proudest bastard, failure is failure but failure after nursing . . . He'll rip the tit away and slit this baby's throat. Three weeks?"

A flash of lightning happened—that's how it seemed to Christopher. Paul was more practised but not enough to avoid the photograph. Basil saw it coming and bundled the three of them into the taxi he had kept waiting at the kerbside. Christopher heard snatches of what the reporter would like to have believed were—and would certainly report as—conversation.

"Mr. Bannerman . . . Reading the reviews . . . ?

"Yes, isn't it bizarre?"

"Can I have a statement . . . ?"

"No".

"Is it true you wrote *Lady in the Sun* two years ago and tried to get . . . Susan Chase . . . for the lead . . . Mr. Bannerman . . . ?"

The taxi was on its way up Fleet Street.

"Bastards" said Basil. "Sorry, Imogen".

"Not at all. I agree".

"Albany first, driver" Basil called through the window behind Christopher.

"Know what?" said Paul.

"What?"

"If your darling weren't ill and asleep and dreaming of being *Lady in the Mountain* . . . I'd like like hell to go and cry on her shoulder".

"She'll be livid when I tell her. Why didn't he wake me, she'll say. We saw worse than this at Cassino said the bleedin' Colonel . . ."

"That's why he collected the M.C. At Cassino, it took

143

time but we got the bloody objective. I don't see the analogy, sir. Said the Captain . . ."

"So the objective gets us. If I may remind you, the objective at Cassino was a ruin by the time we moved in. So, we are 'got' by a ruin. We shall rise like the Phoenix, given a play. Give us a play".

"I'm opting out".

"Oh? How out?"

"Hollywood. I signed a contract last week. They can't tear it up now, I still have one hit running. I go into the money".

"You're a lucky sod. Can't I go too and act for money?"

"If you ask me, yes. But I don't cast, I merely write. And others rewrite, I gather . . ."

"Do you mean you're deserting the theatre?" asked Imogen.

"Come again, little girl?"

"You think it deserted you?"

"That would put it conceitedly—but accurately, see 'tonight' ".

"You'll come right back, sir . . ." said Christopher.

"Do stop 'sirring' me, it bores the . . ."

"Arse off him" Basil completed.

"Yes".

"Paul . . ." said Christopher.

"Yes?"

"If you leave . . . Who the hell is going to captain the side?"

"What side?"

"He's talking like a grown-up" said Basil. "Answer the question".

"What side?"

"The side of the washed folk who want to laugh, you said they'll never stop wanting to".

"Have to do a lot of waiting and seeing. They may laugh at something new. Like babies being throttled in the cradle . . . We don't know, you see. We don't know. And we have to know. I shall sit it out in the sun".

"And let your genius get gangrene?" Basil asked.

"My gangrene . . ." Paul said . . . ". . . may get genius . . ."

They stopped at the Albany entrance and exchanged wishes . . . for what, they couldn't have guessed. Paul walked away from them and Christopher didn't know that he had seen him for the last time.

"What do you think of this profession I profess to belong to?" Christopher asked.

"Challenging" said Imogen. "At this stage, listening to Paul, it's at its most challenging. I thought you were wonderful tonight . . ." she added.

They were in Imogen's . . . 'flat' he would call it. He, Christopher, had a flat—unfinished but promising, during the days since his return to London he had been happy to smell the build-up. His would be fully ready in a fortnight, he had chosen the colours, given opinions. Unneeded. Imogen was a very good imaginer indeed and, for her, the workmen worked. She had a way with people, a way with colours, materials. She began to have a way with Christopher. It was comfort again, whenever it appeared as a possible host he accepted the invitation readily. He could be happy, he decided without hesitation, being a ponce. Upon society, upon those who found him to be stimulating, charming. Upon Imogen . . . ?

He sipped her coffee and the Courvoisier she produced and poured into balloon glasses . . . A cut above the days of Mrs. What-was-her-bloody-name? Twenty-five bob a week, indeed! Who cared, she had gone. They had a man, now. Polite, efficient. He and his wife would occupy the top flat when the conversion was complete, for the moment he cleaned their two flats and swept up the brick dust in the not yet carpeted passages. His service—and that of his wife, later—would not be an extra. There were only two flats occupied. They were alone now in the tall, solid edifice and the walls would not allow the sound of cannon to pass. He thought of shooting cannon. Big Christopher guns, was Imogen ready for the sex? He had been too preoccupied

145

since Jackie but, following the emotional release of the evening, he was prepared for other releases.

She attracted him in a new way. She was neatness, cleanliness, perfection of dress, hair, body . . . A too perfection that he began to want to break down. As, in the near past, he had wanted to invade virginity he was longing now, he realised, to enter perfection, to root about in it and to ravage. Virginity? He didn't think, quite, no. He had not the older ravager's sure judgement of the intacta. But, something . . .

"Wasn't Basil marvellous?" he heard himself saying. What he wanted to say was "Tell me more about me . . . Give me more of the perfection, don't put a beautiful foot wrong . . ." Every reaction, every comment from her had the finish of the finest egg-shell, turquoise, non-drip, ever-last, never-chip paint. He had a mind to chip. To prick the everlast with a fine, drip-at-random, any colour, any shell beginning. She was a sand castle par excellence and he yearned to put a foot on it, in it, up it, kick it around, crush it, smooth it.

"Basil was Basil, I've seen him many times . . ."

She hadn't had a hair out of place all evening.

". . . but you were playing your first part . . ." The green eyes glowed with just the right intensity. ". . . and you were wonderful".

"Make-up all right?"

"Couldn't see any".

"That's good. Hear everything?"

"Everything".

"Clothes?"

"Dead right. Especially the scarf".

He had chosen the scarf with great care, arguing with the designer, losing, winning. And Imogen noticed. She bloody well would he thought as he was half way under.

He examined her in detail. The dress was expensive but didn't say so, the neckline low, not too low, low enough.

"You appreciate that I'm on the brink" he said.

"Of what?"

"Who knows—disaster? Merely the end of my first actor's lesson? I pressed my mount beautifully up the hill, expecting

146

to relax and let him take it easy on a long, downhill stretch the other side. Suddenly, there isn't a downhill stretch. There isn't another side, just a brink. You heard Paul— three weeks . . ."

You had to guess at the reason for her rose colouring. His charm? The Courvoisier? Her mouth . . . was a perfect, narrow oval, barely pointed at the corners. Like a child about to ask a question.

She made a statement. "You'll get a new play".

"I wish I had your confidence".

Her thought before speaking was accompanied, often, by a quick intake of breath. It delighted him.

"Turn her round"—she had changed the sex of his metaphoric mount . . . ". . . and you'll have a downhill stretch. Ride into the country, look for a path to take you forward but not so far up. Where there can't be a brink . . ."

The lips remained parted. As though his answer would always be important.

"You're a wise Imogen, aren't you?" he said. "You're right. *Lady in the Sun*. Paul Bannerman . . . It was riding far too high. A nice hard grind—in Repertory, that's what I need . . ."

"Out of London?"

"Out of London".

"Perhaps . . . it won't be necessary. We'll see . . ."

" 'We'?"

"You said I was wise . . ."

The lips, again, still parted. He prepared the kiss with all the technique at his young command. A salute to perfection.

18

The lowered lighting was well judged. The bathroom door, slightly ajar, let in a shaft of stronger light so that, when she appeared again, she was all but silhouetted. He lay naked in her bed and watched her cat-like progress to his side. She switched off the lamp at his left hand and was silhouetted completely. The pink glow from the bathroom suited such a moment. Christopher always liked a touch of lighting. Offstage.

"Christopher . . ." she said. To be sure of his attention? Her long dressing-gown—the shadowed outline of it—loosened and slipped from her body, disappeared from his view. hair framed her face, almost to her shoulders, and he strained to see the red lights in it. There were none. The black figure moved to him, lifted away the covers. He sensed that she was studying his body in the delicate spill of light that hid her, revealed him. He stretched out his arms, his hands meeting the warm skin of her hips. Moving upwards, they were amazed at the narrowness of the waist. With his two index fingers he pencilled the outline of her up and down, up and down . . . A swift movement that blotted out the light and she was beside him, drawing the covers over them both, enclosing them.

Her love-making was tentative, not virginal but with a check on abandon. Her moist body was eager, yet not practised. He entered her without pain for her, it was not a first experience. But a rare one, he guessed she must have had one or two lovers but didn't make a habit. He explored her body, relished it. The utmost of his pleasure lay in the shame he evoked, pleasing her. Non-virgin as she was, it was like ravishing a novice, he exposed her, laid her open . . .

"Christopher!"

A controlled brutality, it was, that brought them both to climax. She resented the exposure, was appalled by it. And was in ecstasy.

They slept deeply but, as the daylight intruded upon them through the half drawn window curtain, he stirred again. He turned towards her, raised himself on an elbow, studied the sleeping face. Slowly, he drew away the bedclothes from her completely, examined her whole body. She lay on her right side and the dip-down to her waist seemed endless, the curve up to her hip too steep to be possible. Her left leg was turned so that the knee touched the bed, hiding her lower hair. He handled her knee, her thigh, drawing the leg down and across until he was able to see the hair. It was red, like the hair on her head. He took her arm now, and turned her so that she lay on her back, facing up to him. Suddenly, she was wide awake . . .

"No!" she said, and came up to a sitting position, one hand across her large breasts, the other covering herself below. "No . . ."

"Darling . . ." he said, gently. He pressed her down, his own body near to hers, hiding her nakedness for her. "Why are you so shy? This wasn't . . . was it? The first time?"

"Only . . . once before. And I promised myself not again for a long time . . ."

"Has it been a long time?"

"Too long. But . . . treat me gently. You . . . you know so much more . . ."

He folded her in his arms then, releasing her, kissed her breasts, between them, below them . . . At each meeting with his lips her body was in a torment of shame-pleasure. He covered them both with the sheets and kissed her lower body until she cried out to him . . .

"Not . . . not too much, Christopher. Please. Love me, just love me . . ."

He entered her and, this time, the love-making was less tentative. Still, enormously, he drew pleasure from her re-

149

luctance to unbridle. And he was more brutal, laid her shame wider open.

The train was drawing in to Sutton and Christopher realised that he must get a move on with his revision to finish the novel before he reached Victoria. He had revised it so often, how much did this last revision matter? How many times can you dot a set number of 'i's—for that was what this read through amounted to. There was nothing to be done about the text as such . . .

D. Gray had put aside his book and was reading *The Times* again. It had been quite another, smaller evening newspaper that had carried the picture of Paul. He bought the *Star* on his way to the theatre and saw it spread across four columns. The news item was headed 'AUTHOR COULDN'T WAIT'. The item read:

'Author Paul Bannerman—whose play, *Lady in the Sun* was booed last night in London—paid an early morning visit to Fleet Street to read the critical reaction. It was unanimously unfavourable. "Isn't it bizarre?" said Mr. Bannerman, referring to his eagerness to learn whether or not he had yet another hit. Questioned about the rumour that he had written the play two years ago for his close friend Susan Chase, the author made no reply. He got quickly into a waiting taxi and made his exit'.

The review below was devastating in its destruction . . . 'Time the rich Mr. Bannerman learned that there are poorer worlds where ladies do not lie in the sun—not in the French Riviera sun, at all events. They are lucky to get it at Lansbury's Lido . . .'

Christopher had never heard of Lansbury. And he had noted that, nowadays, a yearly spell in the continental sun was within the financial reach of even the 'help' who had been a hindrance at Cornwall Place. Of course, she had knocked up quite a sum tax free. But many did. He didn't decry it, really. He wished he had the knack . . .

Lady in the Sun closed after four weeks—Jackie's play

150

followed them in—and the family broke up for all time. The Templars came to a matinée during the last week—his foster-father had been ill. He looked frail but congratulated Christopher on his debut, was proud of him he said.

"How are funds?"

"I'm all right, thank you very much".

"You wouldn't be silly and not let me know?"

"I promise. But I'm sure I shall be all right. I've written to the Birmingham Repertory Theatre. Mr. Smart gave me an introduction . . ."

"He looks like a good man".

"He is, he's been wonderful to me".

"Good. Good. One thing I'm sure of, Chris, . . . you chose the right job, you have the talent, there's no question. A matter of pegging away . . ."

"You'll get right to the top, my son" said Mrs. Templar. She used the words, always, like a name.

"Thank you. Thank you both, it was kind of you to come".

"Robert wanted to get up out of bed for your first night, I almost had to strap him down. He doesn't like to be bossed, you know".

"I know. Thank God he's in good hands. Take great care of him . . ."

"I will, son. He's all I have left".

"He'd like to think so but you still have me you know".

He saw gratitude in her eyes and put his arms about them both.

He left a ticket, by arrangement, for his own father who neglected to pick it up. Having read the notices?

A fortnight after the closing , Basil took Cecily to Montreux. He telephoned Christopher in the morning.

"Nothing lined up, old lad?"

"No. The tour I told you about has been cancelled. I'm still waiting to hear from the Birmingham Rep. . . ."

"Listen. Telephone the B.B.C. . . . better still, write, they love words on paper . . . Leslie Joyce . . . he's a producer, knows me . . . Mention my name, he'll arrange for you to give an audition . . . Not much but it might keep the wolf away".

151

"I'm awfully grateful . . ."

"Feel guilty about letting you in for a flop . . ."

"What nonsense! I . . ."

"If you'd written to Birmingham when you left the Reid Foster you'd have got in. You'd be set for the autumn".

"How's Cecily?"

"Top form. Fighting form, she's been fighting me about the trip again. Thinks we should save the money . . ."

"Well . . ."

" 'Balls' I said and 'Balls' I meant. One life. Short. Montreux, that's it, got to show her who's master. Write to Joyce . . . And get on with that play of yours, don't sit on your arse".

"I won't. Have a marvellous time".

"Send you a postcard. You keep me posted too. About that gipsy fellow I played with in New York . . . Doesn't apply to me, I'm rare. Don't lose my *Galatea*, I want it back . . ."

Birmingham replied that the company was engaged already. If they thought of making a change, they would let him know.

Over the weeks that followed, Christopher earned a little from small parts in three radio plays. He took the thin basic story, too, from his stage play and wrote it for the microphone. It was accepted after two more re-writes and he saw, for the first time, his name in print as author. He played the second lead in it and the deal, overall, brought him nearly a hundred pounds so that he was able to breathe, with a little difficulty, financially. He continued to live in Imogen's house, in his own flat. Paying the earlier rent, she insisted, until he made some small killing. He thought the radio play fitted this bill but she would not agree.

"Don't be a fool, darling. I have every flat in the building let and I don't reckon to make money out of you. In any event, I don't believe in your need to recompense me. Did you never hear of patronage?"

Christopher had.

"I believe in you" she went on. "And any small help I can give you is nothing if peace of mind allows you to create a play. A book . . ."

Christopher had thought much about writing a novel if he could find a story that fired him. In the deep back of his mind, there had been born an idea—unwanted. He had stifled it at birth.

As he lay, one night, in her bed she called out to him from the bathroom . . . "You were saying . . . you wanted to write a novel . . ."

"Not so easy" he called to her. "I'd like to try out the technique of it but I haven't an idea in my head for a story".

"I have".

"What did you say?"

"I said I have. An idea for a story. A real life story. You'd make it fiction of course, disguise the characters, but as a story it's . . . almost too dramatic to be true. But it's true all right. It's up to you to write it credibly. That . . . wouldn't be so easy . . ."

"What story?"

"The one they serialised in the Sunday papers some months back. When you were touring with *Lady in the Sun*. They wrote it sketchily. And for sensation, you'd have to go to the original newspaper files to find the truth. Daddy could help. He knows all sorts of people in Fleet Street . . ."

"What . . . story?"

It was the thought born unwanted, he knew. It had to be.

"Susan Something-or-other. That film star who was . . . Chase . . . You know . . . Paul's . . ."

He heard only a murmur from her, no distinguishable words. The thought he had stifled had begun to breathe again, it came bounding into his consciousness to ally itself with the thoughts expressed that filled the air about him. He sat up, she was still talking.

"Imogen!"

She came into the room and looked at him in surprise.

"Paul?"

"You can't possibly be serious".

"About the novel? Of course, why?"

"Paul is . . ."

153

"Hardly your friend, is that what you were going to say?"

"He's . . . I like him. He's Basil's friend, I couldn't do it. To either of them".

"I don't see why not. If you're going to be a writer, write an important book, the subject matter, its validity, your treatment of it are your real concern".

"And the feelings of others? Of people I like?"

"I happen to think they are secondary. If you're really going to create something worthwhile. These are events that took place. Dig deep into them, find out why and relate them with your own comment in your style".

He lay beside her. She had not yet become accustomed to being exposed to him emotionally. Nor even physically, he had never seen her naked in the light, only in the near darkness. On the nights when he shared with her, she was careful to draw the curtains close across the window to keep out the dawn. And, always, she wore her dressing-gown until she was near to the bed. In the half light.

Now, she made a movement to caress him. It was for him to be shamed and he turned away from her.

"Christopher . . ."

"I'm . . . tired . . . Goodnight".

She made no further reference to the idea of a novel based upon Susan Chase. It was Christopher who brought it up again . . .

"You said your father had friends in Fleet Street".

"Yes".

"Would you . . . arrange something? I want to read the newspapers—all of them if I can—published in nineteen thirty four . . . about . . .

"I'll get on to it right away".

He researched, made notes, began writing. But he would never read to her what he had written, nor even discuss it. He talked about his new radio play, of a play for the theatre he was thinking of drafting . . .

He had begun to despair of ever again setting foot on

a stage until, one day, a letter arrived from the Neil Lamont office. Mr. Lamont was casting a play to be directed by St. John Pender and, if Christopher cared to, he might present himself for an audition. He was elated, so was Imogen and she broached a development in patronage.

"You should have a new suit".

"I can't afford it".

"I can and you're to go to Daddy's tailor and be measured today. I'll get him to telephone them, they'll do it in the time".

"But . . ."

"Darling. If you don't look right you won't feel right. And if you don't feel right, you won't give out that Tighson charm that made me fall in love with you".

"What did you say?"

"If I did, I shouldn't have, you should first. I'll get the tailor . . ."

Christopher arrived early. At two thirty five for three p.m. Clad in his first Savile Row suit, it hung like a close cut worsted dream and bloody well should. He had asked, discreetly, the price at his final fitting and nearly landed himself with the bill. The head cutter told him—he was a partner in the firm and his answer conveyed that he was unused to discussing matters of price. He had added . . .

"But I understood from Miss Walker . . ."

"That's all right, yes. I just . . . It's very good".

"Thank you, sir" had been the frigid closure. Christopher did ask himself whether he should not have written a cheque but the old acceptor of comfort within him had forbidden it. Would it have been honoured? Just about. Success was coming up again, surely, easier to wait. Easier.

The auditions were to be held at the theatre where *Lady in the Sun* had been booed and where Jennie's play was now running. (It had not replaced *Cloth of Gold*—the Royals had boosted that into success, they still rated higher than the mufflers). He felt like a stranger as he passed through the stage door. The same man kept the door—the man he had tipped on four successive Saturdays, instructed to do so by Basil.

"Name?"

"I'm Christopher Tighson . . ."

"Oh. Oh, yes. You know the way down to the stage?"

"Of course".

"Down you go, then".

When mufflers were in would tipping be out, he wondered.

He waited in the wings while another actor read. He had collected a script two days earlier and knew the scene by heart. But he would read it to be on the safe side. It was a very different play from *Lady in the Sun*. A straight piece by a new author—Christopher had seen his photograph (no tie) in The Stage. He couldn't—but must, perhaps?—pretend that it was brilliant. The setting was a North Country town where the son of a rich father drew envy from his co-workers for unearned promotion. It was too obvious a comment. Shaw was not yet born again.

The boy on the stage was giving a lisping interpretation of the part which was written as a virile public school man. No competition there, he thought. He whispered to the Assistant Stage Manager . . .

"How many are reading for this part?"

"Only this one and you, duckie".

Oh, Christ. He was, at once, in the middle again of that damned party, waiting for the overture by Sookie. What grudge was he bearing? None at all, he had signed the letter, hadn't he? Inviting him to the audition? 'Dear Christopher . . . Kind regards, Neil Lamont'. Not 'Sookie', but then he wouldn't sign himself 'Sookie' . . .

The boy finished his reading and, holding his script to

shade away the foot-lighting, peered out into blackness.
Christopher heard a voice—St. John's—say . . .

"Thank you, Robbie. Would you be a darling and wait
. . . ?"

Christopher got a stray whiff of scent as the boy minced
past him into the darkness of the wings.

"Christopher Tighson?" said the Stage Manager who had
read with the mincing boy. And Christopher walked con-
fidently on to the stage. He had expected to feel at home.
This was, after all, his theatre, the one in which he had
created a part in a Paul Bannerman play and got eight
laughs. He learned that nothing is more dismissive than the
fall of a final curtain and the striking of a set. A voice
greeted him from the orchestra rail.

"Good afternoon, Christopher".

It was Sookie.

"Good afternoon, sir".

"My, we are formal. But then, it has been a long time,
hasn't it?" He called over his shoulder "He looks older,
doesn't he St. John?"

"A little" St. John obeyed.

"You've read the play?"

"Yes".

"Do you like it?"

"It's very interesting . . ."

"It's a good part. Would you like to play it?"

"Very much".

"Well, we'll see, shall we? Dazzle us with a scene, Simon
will read it with you . . ."

"It's on page forty three" ventured St. John.

"He knows that, he's been listening, haven't you, Christopher?"

"Er . . . yes".

"And you're confident, aren't you? Right down your
street, the part, don't you think?"

"Yes . . . I . . ."

"Dazzle us".

Christopher read well, he was sure. There was a silence
after he had spoken the last speech and he waited. Terrified
but strangely confident. He wasn't in sympathy with the

mood of the play but he had sunk himself into the disagree-
able outburst which expressed the author's view. Not his
view but this was what acting was about. He had certainly
played the mincing boy out into the alley, he knew it, knew
it. The silence continued, unbearably. Then Sookie sauntered
from his stalls seat down to the orchestra rail.

"You certainly read that well" he said and called back
to St. John who hadn't left his seat "Didn't he read well,
St. John? Gave us quite an idea, didn't he . . . ?"

"Thank you" Christopher said.

Sookie looked long at him, the sadness of the face raped
by the dancing eyes. Like an undertaker screaming a modern
song.

" 'Tisn't . . ." he said . . . "quite enough, though—is it?"
(Turning again and calling). "Not enough" he said to Christopher ". . . to give us an idea. What a pity!"

"But . . . Would you . . . ? I'll read again".

"I'm sure you will. Sweet of you".

The eyes burned as they danced, Christopher thought
you could have lit a cigarette at them.

"Thank you, no" Sookie concluded. "Let's say you lost
the part . . . on a technicality".

"A . . . ? I don't . . ."

Sookie had turned away and was walking back up the
aisle. St. John called out to Christopher . . .

"Thank you. I'm sorry".

In a moment, he and Sookie had their heads together in
conversation, excluding him.

He left the stage without a further word said by him or to
him. The Stage Manager held out a hand to receive the
script but avoided his eye. He passed through into the corridor behind the stage and went quickly up the stairs,
through a door marked 'Gents'. He had used the room
before but not to cry in. It was the second time in his
young life that he had cried alone, in a lavatory.

In Shaftesbury Avenue, he met Jackie.

"You look like death".

"I've been to a funeral, maybe the look is catching".

158

"You didn't get the part".

"You knew?"

'I knew you were reading for it. And I knew that Evelyn Coke was reading for it, that meant you wouldn't get it if you were David Garrick".

"If I were David Garrick, I wouldn't need it".

"You poor darling. Would a cup of tea help?"

"I don't think so".

"I could make it tea and a newly laid egg" she said. And, in Shaftesbury Avenue on an October afternoon, they both laughed like idiots and disturbed the passers-by.

They went home to Jackie's and combed, with close teeth, the change that had come over the theatre. And other changes—like Sookie—that might have come over it but hadn't. In an artistic revolution, it is never the heads of managers that fall.

"We come off in four weeks" Jackie said.

"The notice is up?"

"Not yet but it will be".

Jackie knew more about what was going on and coming off than most and most knew more than Christopher.

"I thought you were a success".

"We have the aura. Sookie papers the house like mad, he doesn't like to see empty seats. But, in the end, it's the people who tell Sookie, he hates that. What's new with Basil?"

"I had a card from him. He went to Montreux, Cecily was ill . . ."

"I knew. But he's back now, surely?"

"I telephoned him only last week and somebody else answered. He's moved".

"Where to?"

"They didn't know".

"There're bound to at 'Spotlight' . . ."

"I . . . must try them. I hope he's all right. That Cecily's all right, I mean".

Jackie didn't answer. Tea was ready.

Over tea, she told him that Paul had scripted his play— the one that was still packing houses in London—for the screen.

159

"They hope to get Audrey Hepburn" she said.

"I wonder if Paul is happy".

"With all that Californian sun and the lolly too? Mind you, Hollywood must have its ghosts for him. Or, one ghost. Did you think he was queer?"

"Paul? No!"

"You're very emphatic. That might mean he tried it with you and didn't make it and you're really saying *you're* not".

"I don't follow".

"Skip it. More tea?"

"No. Thank you".

"Did you have it off with Liane?"

"What? I . . . Don't be . . . What do you mean?"

"I had a feeling you did. Nothing to be incoherent about, it's a feather in your cap and I don't mean 'cap'. She certainly left her marks on you".

"I . . ."

"Don't play the innocent with me. You're a nice tall, lean, stiff hunk of a man, Chrissie, and I'm glad you didn't get the part. 'Job' I mean. Well, both. Shall we go to bed?"

They did, and Christopher needed to take no initiative. She stripped him, drank him, and all but ate him in the two tiring hours that followed. She caressed every inch of his body and drew from him the desire to explore her. This was an increasing thirst in him and he found, with Jackie certainly, that by employing tactics strange and hitherto unconsidered he could satisfy her and retain his own urge. With nymphos, the conservation of ammunition is the preservation of the man image. And they are so easily, for the moment, satisfied. Christopher learned.

It was past eleven o'clock. She had made a meal for him—having made one of him, he reflected as she cooked—and they sat drinking coffee. Christopher thought he knew how a bee must feel having stung with his barbed sting, pulled away and been disembowelled. Mind you, it was pleasant. A pleasant disembowelment but you needed, in fine, your bowels.

"Let's go out" Jackie said.

"Out?"

In and out, what did women want of nice, tall, lean, stiff men? Stiff. What was that then, he strove to remember?

They danced at a club Jackie belonged to. A rather select club—which suggests that you select the club. It selected you. And milked you in every other remaining way.

They danced cheek-to-cheek, scorning the new style—the face-to-face-but-don't-touch that was beginning to be the way for some. The music didn't invite it.

"Hello, old Chris . . ."

The voice was warm, not of tea and nymphomania and tired dinner and whacked cheek to cheeking. Christopher was very drunk.

"What?"

Basil, it was, playing the quiet, defiant piano.

"Basil!"

"Don't attract attention, old son. On duty".

Suddenly, Christopher's eyes filled with tears, the alcohol didn't help concealment. "What are you . . . ?"

"Doing? Earning. Man can't live by depicting these days. Man has a gift, man uses. How's tricks?" He continued to play a very adroit piano and Jackie chatted and Christopher slurred a remark or two. Basil stopped playing.

Christopher was at the table with them and Basil was telling them that Cecily was well and at home and that that's where he, Basil would be soon. He, Christopher, remembered no more. Until they entered his flat.

"All right, then?" Basil said.

"Where's Jackie?"

"Sent her home. Each to his own and all that. Want me to put you to bed?"

"Balls".

"Quite so. Any man who can't put himself to bed should lie on the covers. Clean your teeth".

"What?"

"Your teeth. Clean 'em. Where's your toothbrush?"

"In the . . . I can . . . No man can clean the teeth of another man" Christopher said.

"Well spoken. So. Clean the buggers".

161

Basil stood by while this was done and, having seen Christopher stretched on the bed . . .

"Trousers off?"

"On. Never take 'em off again. Determined" said Christopher.

"Good maxim".

"Maximal".

"What? Never mind. Goodnight, old thing. No need to say 'sleep well'. One touch of Jackie makes the whole world. Sleep. Thank God she's clean. 'Night . . ."

" 'Night".

The door opened and that must mean Imogen, oh Christ. She had his key and he hers. It was her building anyway, why shouldn't she have a key? To his flat, to his drawers —wooden and sartorial . . . To his Savile Row suit . . . Give it back? You can't and he didn't want to. The door opened . . .

"Chris?"

" 'Mm?"

"Darling. You didn't get it".

"Get it? Get . . . what?"

"The part".

"Part, what part?'

"You went for an audition, remember?"

"Nineteen years ago. Didn't get it. David Garrick got it. I'm drunk".

"I know and I don't blame you".

"Imogen . . ."

"Yes?"

"Don't be so bloody perfect. Mind you . . . I love it . . . Perfect . . . Imogen . . ."

"Yes?"

"Would you . . . please . . . take off my clothes?"

"Of course".

She did.

Next morning, late, she cooked breakfast for him in his flat and made dark black coffee.

Later, when he was quite conscious, she said . . .

162

"You did the best thing. Got drunk".

"Yes. Did I? Do the best thing, I mean?"

"You did. I wouldn't blame you, either, if you went to bed with the first girl you saw . . ."

"I did".

"Don't . . . tell me. I don't blame you but I don't want to know".

"Imogen . . ."

"Yes?"

"You're too bloody perfect".

"You said that last night, I'm not. I just . . . happen to love you and I understand. If she gave you comfort, I'm glad she was there".

"That's too perfect".

"It isn't true either, really, but it's the best I can do . . ."

"You're crying".

"Of course I am".

"Because I slept with another girl? She didn't mean a thing except . . . comfort . . ."

"No".

"What?"

"I'm crying because I'm your patron. And you didn't get the job".

"I didn't" he said. "But it's going to make good copy".

Her eyes were aglow, suddenly. "For your novel? That's the way, use it!"

Use it. From now on, he thought, I'm going to use everything and everybody, if it's bitch eat dog, I'm going to switch it back. And I'm going to make the biggest, most satisfying meal-of-a-bitch dog ever made.

Over the next two months Christopher completed his story line and began, three times, to write the novel. Three times he abandoned it, telling himself that the need to carry on with his more urgent career, earn money at it, was the reason. In fact, he had accepted the patronage offered, liked the soft cushion, leaned back on it. He neither liked nor could accept, readily, the tear-down of Paul. The story would wear a heavy disguise but recognition would be immediate by the few. 'Any similarity between the character of the homosexual and Paul Bannerman is purely . . .' He knew—or

163

thought he knew—that Paul was not a homosexual. But it suited the framework he planned for his narrative. A near homosexual pushed over the line after rejection by this fame hooked youngster . . . 'Any similarity between the actress and Susan Chase . . .' It was like taking little waxen images of those whom you knew—he now thought he knew Susan—and, not sticking pins into them, but twisting them slowly, painfully—for you, for them?—into grotesques. Not far distant from the malice of plush, bar gossip. Destruction. But stylish destruction, 'Relate it with your own comment in your style . . .' The playwright, in his story, was brilliant. But his first opportunities came from sources not over influenced by the brilliance. Christopher related the Oxford-shire party scene word by word, almost, as it had happened to him. Disguising the character of Lamont only slightly, would there be a lawsuit? At the final, near final, moment, his Paul character succumbed. Thereafter, all doors, all stages, were opened to him and he went to immediate and continuing triumph. In his story there would be ultimate rejection, again, by the Lamont character. The inference to be drawn . . . that the sell-out of integrity will lead to a sell-out of you by the success you sold out for. Muddled? But he would sort it. If only he could bring himself to begin and, this time, not abandon.

In December, he began again and Imogen paid a thousand pounds into his bank account. He accepted both events like a medicinal dose.

CHAPTER

20

At Christmas he travelled north with Imogen to meet and stay with her parents. Sam Walker was 'in wool'. He had made his comfort by knowing more about sheep and the way to shear both them and the buyers. As Sookie knew how to shear actors and playwrights for the over paying sitters in the seats. The sheep could be certain of growing another saleable coat, there was the difference, and you had to feed them or no coat. The actor was not so sure. Nor the playwright whose main safety lay in lack of numbers. Thinking so, Christopher could have wished he had been 'called' into wool.

He liked Sam Walker, upon whom there were no flies and who made no bones—using such clichés if he felt like them—about telling you what was what.

"So this is the lad all t' fuss is about" he said when they met, summing Christopher up in half one. "Big bugger, isn't he?"

"You must forgive my husband" said Mrs. Walker. She was high born and beautiful and the kind of mate many a Sam Walker had been known to aspire to. Yet, she seemed to love him. Or like him, respect him. Her attitude reminded Christopher of the perfection of her daughter's behaviour. Mrs. Walker smiled a correct smile, laying her hand on Sam's arm, using just the right amount of pressure.

"Always call a spade a spade" he said. "Do you hunt, young fella?"

"Er . . . no, I never have".

"Then I don't advise you to start now, it's hell on the underparts. Don't disapprove of blood sports though, I hope?"

"No, sir".

"That's right, lad. Can't abide a hypocrite. All those high-minded folk who write to the papers about killing a poor bloody fox . . . they spend the rest of their time doing each other to death. I should think, at a guess, you're in a blood sport yourself, am I right?"

"Sir?"

"Actors and the like? They're no less cannibals than the rest of us, are they? Dog eat dog?"

Christopher thought of the novel he was planning to write. And, in writing, joining the eaters. "Its . . . pretty hard going".

"Stick at it, lad. Toughest dog with biggest appetite wins. No reason why it shouldn't be you".

Sam was short and built like a bull. The red face had two small grey eyes set in it and they pierced through Christopher to the very thought in the back of his head.

"Sense enough to have a second string, I hear. Bit of a writer?"

"I try to be".

"That's not the answer. Give me a plain 'yes', I'll think more of you".

"Yes . . ."

"Sam, darling", said Mrs. Walker, "don't be hard on Christopher. He doesn't know you yet".

"He will. He will".

The house was vast but, in contrast to Sookie's, old and beautiful. Elizabeth, with Queen Anne—even Regency— additions. It had belonged, surely, to Claire's family and any crumbling that might have been in process would have been halted at once by the ton-load cement-solidarity of Sam and his sheep. It was a match of deep necessity from both partners, Christopher decided. Now, from the gravel in the driveway and the well kept gardens to the controlled warmth of the interior with its superb furnishings, all was a fortress of well-being. If revolution spread from the theatre to industry they'd be hard put to it to hang a second muffler round the neck of Sam Walker.

The hunt met next day and Imogen and her mother rode off, leaving Sam and Christopher watching from the huge arched doorway.

"I had a go, you know" Sam said. "But not for long. My bum wasn't brought up to it. You and me can have a long talk later before they get back. Once they do, they'll go over whole bloody hunt, hedge by hedge, they're worse than golfers. Let me show you the house".

The story was as Christopher had guessed. Moreover, Sam was disposed to tell most of it freely and with pride.

"Very old family" he said. "On their uppers when I came along".

They had moved from the hall into the long Elizabethan room with its minstrel gallery. Christopher looked at the parade of portraits.

"Won't find many of my ancestors up there. All Claire's.

166

They go back to t' Conqueror. Ugly looking lot. Till you come down this end . . . What about that, then?"

It was a portrait—Christopher thought, by Van Dyck—of a group of children.

"Buckingham family" Sam said. "Kid on the left, she's a cousin of first Duke of Buckingham. Claire's her direct descendant, what do you think o' that, eh? See the likeness?" Christopher had no hesitation in saying that he did. The high forehead, the set of the head, the eyes . . . Claire—or Imogen—in infancy . . .

"Takes your breath away, doesn't it? And look at this one over here. This is much later, Sir Joshua Reynolds. Could be Claire?"

"Yes. Or Imogen".

"Very like her mother is Imogen. When she was born, I was in a blue funk for fear she'd grow up to look like me".

"Oh . . ."

"Don't say owt daft. Mind you, I wasn't so dusty myself when I were young. Touch on the short side but I had many a lass on my tail. She grew up the spit and look of her mother, thank God. Nature knew which side her bread was buttered . . ."

He turned his back on the portrait and stood for a moment with his eyes tight closed.

"First met my Claire in this very room . . . I was a city Alderman. We ran a big charity do in Town Hall and some of us got invited up here for dinner first. Bloody awful food. I could see right away how things were. Place was as cold as a morgue and it hadn't seen a brush of paint for twenty years . . ." His eyes came open and looked high above him. "There was a patch of damp round that chandelier you could have grown mushrooms in. All through t' meal I were wond'ring if ceiling were going to come down . . . Tradition. Got to keep it dry, lad, it's worth keeping dry. Nothing to put in its place, you see. That's what's the matter with the French, they chopped the heads off all their aristocrats and what have you got? A nation of money-grubbers. Like me. It's up to the Sam Walkers to make the foundations solid and keep 'em that way. That's what we're best at. But we don't half like to see a bit of style. And the best of us know how to appreciate it".

They went through room after room and Sam pointed out every feature that was not of his world but that his world needed. It seemed to Christopher that he regarded the re-instatement as a privilege granted him by the luck of his having been present at a poor meal in a run-down house-hold, the privilege a prize he had gained against a possible later comer.

"Lucky I saw it first" he said. I had a word with Claire's father on the way to the ball. Invited myself up again next day—something of vital importance to discuss, I told him. It was Claire, you see. I couldn't abide to see a picture like that in a rotting frame. I got to talking to her. Now, whether it was me wanting to help out that led to other feelings . . . or it might have been t'other way round . . . Love's a funny bugger . . ."

Later, they sat in the library—in the Queen Anne part of the house. And Christopher felt that grace and beauty were constants, not to be disturbed by pettifogging impermancies. But they needed their champions. Sam asked him . . .

"What's this between you and my Imogen?"

"We . . . we're very close . . . at present".

"What do you mean 'at present'?"

"I'm trying to be honest . . ."

"That suits me".

"I don't know . . . whether I'm capable of staying close. To one person".

"That's a fair statement. Not had a lot of time to find out, have you? She loves you, you know". Sam used the word firmly but you knew he was on intimate terms with its kin-ships.

"I know. And I'm grateful that she does. I just . . . don't want to let her down".

"She's a clever girl".

"Yes".

"She's put that house of hers to rights . . ."

"It's marvellous what she has done".

"She wants to put your house to rights too, how do you feel about that?"

"It's . . . a strange thing. I want to make a success and Imogen wants to help me . . ."

"She is helping you".

The grey eyes searched him for thoughts held back.

"Yes. Do you think I shouldn't allow her to?" Sam screwed up his eyes and looked at Christopher with head cocked to one side.

"Depends" he said. "She believes in you. Whether you should accept her help or not depends on how much you believe in yourself. Physically, Imogen is like her mother. In every other way . . . she's like her Dad. That means she's determined, ruthless when she wants something enough. She wants you".

"That doesn't mean she has to buy me" said Christopher suddenly. He added "I'm sorry".

"Don't be sorry for saying what you mean. I give you credit". Sam went through a washing of his face movement with one hand. "Money" he said . . . "It's something you have to think right about. I've got it, Claire hasn't. Or hadn't. But, you see, I used it to put the damp course round this building. Now it's rock-solid. She is, I am, that's the way to use money. Claire is a wonderful woman. I wanted her more than anything in the whole world. You could say I bought her".

"Oh . . . but . . ."

"Don't talk cock, lad. Cards on the table with me, that's the way. Claire has got a very soft spot for me. And a loyalty that's akin to love, I don't ask more. Imogen won't ask more of you if she's got sense and she has".

"Oh, Christ. . . !"

"Lad?"

"You suggest poncing is a way of life to be commended?"

"Don't use that word to me, youngster . . ."

"I'm sorry".

"You're not and no reason to be. But I don't see it your way. It's a simple matter of how little you're prepared to take . . . and how much of your deep down guts you're prepared to give. A ponce, as I understand it, gives bugger-all".

There was a long pause during which Sam poured two

of the stiffest whiskies Christopher had ever seen—in huge, heavy glasses.

"Happy Christmas".

"Happy Christmas, sir".

They drank and Sam walked to his chair and sat again, continuing to subject his guest to shameless scrutiny.

"Do you have parents?" he asked at last.

"A father, yes. And . . . sort of foster-parents, they looked after me during the war".

"See 'em often?"

"Not as often as I should".

"In the normal way, you'd spend Christmas with 'em? Or with your father?"

"My father is retired. He leads his own life and it doesn't really include me".

"Don't you mean you've cut him off?"

"No I don't, sir. My mother I got on with, she died a few years ago. My foster-parents are wonderful people. Ordinarily, I spend time with them. Some time".

"Christmas?"

"Christmas, yes".

"Not this Christmas".

"Not this Christmas, I wrote to them to explain".

They drank in silence and Christopher surveyed the collection of books that surrounded them. The question that came into his mind received immediate answer . . .

"Apart from the reference books I've read every one, cover to cover, at least once".

"You have a wonderful library".

"You'll know all about it, taking a degree and all . . ."

I'll bet he has a bloody file on me, Christopher thought.

"Bit of eye trouble, I hear. Kept you out of doing your National Service".

"Yes Glaucoma. Nothing like as serious as it sounds. Sort of poor circulation in the eye".

"Kept you out of the Army, though?"

"Yes. I was very thankful it did. If the war had still been on, I wouldn't have been, but the way things were I was glad".

"What do you do for it?"

"I use eye-drops three times a day. It keeps it in check, you can't cure it. But it doesn't worry you at all".

"What do you mean, if the war had been on you wouldn't have been glad?"

"Well . . . I wouldn't have wanted to be out when everybody else was in".

"I could have pulled a string or two, I suppose. I was over forty. But I didn't. I was damned glad when they shoved me into Supply, though. There's a fellow round here, a brigadier, covered in medals. Born hero, every step of the way from Anzio to Berlin. Then he got his fundaments shot off. You're right lad. I wouldn't have wanted to be out of it. But I'm bloody glad I weren't in it up to my fundaments. Poor sod". Sam peered deeply into his glass as though hoping to glimpse there an assurance that fundaments would never again be in jeopardy. A land fit for fundaments to live in . . .

Christopher took in the books once more. How many masterpieces made up the accepted canon? Did a writer have to aim, always, at a masterpiece or could he just write? He rose and carried his drink in the direction of the longest, most imposing line of volumes 'XXVI' said the last. Dickens. A wealth of 'comment in your style'. About a yard and a half of it, he thought. Twenty six volumes, each filled with style, comment, perdurable character. What a world he had been born into, though! Fertile in evil.

"Great books" said the voice behind him. Sam had risen and was, again, in pursuit. "They did good, too. Mind you, in his day there was a lot of good to be done . . ." The thought-reader. Christopher thanked God he didn't have to do business with him. Or did he? "We can't all put the world to rights" Sam added.

"No, sir".

"Don't put it to wrong, though".

Christopher turned in surprise. Mercifully, the eyes that made him feel naked were no longer looking. Sam was peering through a window.

"They'll be coming home" he said. Then, turning . . . "Bit of an upheaval going on in your business, my lass tells me. I read the papers, too. New blood coming in?"

"Yes".

"Thank the stars you're young, then. It's the older ones who'll need to watch out. You didn't get that job?"

"No, I didn't".

"There'll be others. Don't let it make you bitter, that's narrowing. Can bring the mind down as thin as a ribbon. One thing I learned before I was twelve. Any time they close the gates on you, hop over the fence. If it's too high, make a hole in the bugger, they can't keep you out if you've a mind to get in".

Without a further word, he took Christopher's glass— Christopher was surprised to find it empty—and refilled for them both. The room had darkened. Sam made no move to put on the lights. He threw a log on the fire and stood with his back to it and Christopher noticed for the first time the portrait of Claire over the mantel. Claire at the age Imogen now was.

"Simon Elwes painted that. There isn't much old Reynolds could teach him. He didn't flatter. Just painted beauty . . ."

"Yes . . ."

"Beauty as it was and is. I sometimes wonder . . . if she'd been the one with the money, whether she'd have chosen me".

He laughed suddenly, a loud but not unpleasant noise that echoed round the room.

"That's a bloody lie" he corrected. "I don't wonder at all". The eyes pierced Christopher again. "It's Christmas Eve" he said.

"Yes".

"Telephone's over there".

"The telephone?"

"Those foster-parents of yours, aren't they on the 'phone?'

"Yes".

"They'll be glad to hear from you".

Christopher had an impulse to invent trouble at the other end of the line. A problem that would give him the excuse to leave. He felt that he was here under a false pretence, as a candidate for membership of a family to whom, soft as were the cushions, he had no intention of returning one day as a son-in-law. Or had he? Imogen would want it, Claire, Sam seemed to like him. He had been open with Sam and had—he thought—endeared himself more than had been his need or want, by the very candour. He was not prepared to let their acceptance of him close off all retreat. If, indeed, he wanted retreat. Time, he wanted. A long time, to know his mind. Was this pushing a pressure to be resisted or was it to be named Fate and given into without fight?

"Are they well, son?"

Son.

"Well. Yes" he said, and the temptation to improvise had been withstood. He knew he couldn't have carried it off with Sam.

"Want to try your father?"

He didn't, but felt that an affirmative would be expected. To his father's number, there was no reply.

There followed a week that Christopher was reluctant to let go. The living that Time owed him, he was certain, for launching him too young into revolution flowed richly around him and over him and he luxuriated in the warmth. He lay as in a bath, inert and with comfort ministered. There were presents, there were parties, there were excursions into the countryside. Meetings with agreeable people. On the eve of the New Year, friends gathered in the house and the champagne in the raised glasses seemed to offer sparkle without end, if he would but drink.

"Good luck, lad".

"Thank you, sir".

"A wonderful New Year" said Claire. And, including Imogen . . . "For you both".

Imogen glowed with her joyous possession of him.

"To you, Christopher" she said.

"To you" he said. "A perfect New Year . . ." He sipped from his glass.

173

21

At Victoria, Christopher was early out of the train. He had not bothered to carry a briefcase, his springback-encased novel was tight under his left arm as he went back to find a door. He stepped on to the platform and began his long walk to the ticket barrier, passing the compartment he had travelled in. D. Gray was there. Adjusting his bowler hat. Their eyes met and Gray's were pathetic in appeal. Christopher was reminded of Liane's passage by his window at Crewe Station. He didn't quite cut dead D. Gray but, as he passed, it was as much a rejection of homo as Liane's passage was a rejection of his hetero. No White Russian at his heels so he was able to quicken his pace.

The Walkers, it seemed—Sam and Imogen—were devotees and masters of reinstatement. Number Eleven, Cornwall Place was itself again. Or, if not quite itself, an acceptable something else. The frontage was four coat painted, the cornice renewed, the shell pittings filled in—medals removed but one couldn't, Christopher appreciated, be proud forever of knocks taken. Imogen remarked, satisfied, that neighbour houses had been shamed into emulation.

"It will send the values up" she commented. Sam would have approved her assessment.

The brass shone round the bell-pushes and beneath—each had its plate giving the name of the dweller and all flats were occupied. As they entered, they trod into deep carpeting. That the housekeeping couple were already in residence could be seen from the spick and span welcome, the green pile tended like a well kept lawn. Even the doorknobs polished, Christopher didn't think the new playwrights would be pleased.

Inside his flat, he came upon the first novelty of the young year. A letter from his father . . .

'Dear Christopher . . .' It was in his father's own careful hand, every word considered. 'You will be surprised to learn that I have re-married. My wife is, quite naturally, anxious to meet you. Will you be kind enough to telephone me at the earliest at my new number (given with the new address, above) and we will arrange a meeting. Perhaps you will dine with us one evening? Do, please, feel at liberty to bring a lady with you to make four. Your devoted father . . .'

"Imogen!" he shouted up the stairs.

Christopher's father had removed to Knightsbridge and they had dinner by candlelight. He was tall, iron grey haired only, and in his early sixties. He had shed—by candlelight, certainly—ten years at least and, as he busied himself with the wines, he threw many a fond glance at his bride who was, at most, forty. John Tighson approved Imogen as he had always approved security. He had a fully developed sensibility of this.

"To the ladies" said Tighson Senior, raising a glass.

"The ladies" Christopher said.

They had met on a cruise only a few weeks earlier. Virginia, the bride, had been married to a baronet who had died ten months ago. Christopher was surprised to assume that his father must have adventured beyond his instincts to travel First. Perhaps he had taken the cruise with a meeting in mind? Travelled First with, in mind, just such a meeting? Suddenly, Christopher was embarrassed by Imogen's presence. Like father, like son, would she feel? For some contrary reason, he gave his father marks not less than full. And he laughed aloud.

"My boy?"

"I was just . . . happy. For you both".

Virginia was charming, attractive in a sly way. She wore a gown that reminded Christopher of the Balmain garment

175

worn by the untalented star of *Lady in the Sun*. At three hundred guineas cost to whoever it was footed Sookie's bills. He knew that the flat and every item in it would be hers. And he still gave his father A's for effort and achievement. A rich, dead baronet and a live, wool-gathering father. The Tighsons were qualifiers in the Ponce Olympics.

Christopher got very drunk.

The second dinner party of this New Year was more to be enjoyed. He took Imogen again, at Basil's invitation, to the club where he had got drunk with Jackie. He was relieved to see that Jackie wasn't there. A slim youth played a less comforting piano.

"Glad to hand that one over" said Basil. "Now . . ." he said, "News! Cecily and I are off to the Antipodes".

"The where? Australia?"

"There speaks a lad who knows his geography. Yes. And the neighbour islands, North and South. It's called New Zealand".

"How splendid!" Imogen said.

Christopher compared the red of Imogen's hair with the Titian of Cecily's. And thought Titian the more exciting. Cecily looked completely well and radiant. Something about older women, he thought . . . Basil was chatting on.

"The New Wave has yet to roll in on Bondi Beach, you see. Before it does, I'm going in two plays—both by old Paul. London's most stubborn success . . . And . . ."

"Not . . ?"

"*Lady in the Sun*? Yes. Sorry, old drugget, nothing for you. They have supporting actors even in Australia, I'm told. They only travel the stars. Stars, what am I saying? But they're shoving me above the title and they're travelling me. You wouldn't come, anyway . . ."

"Wouldn't I!" He caught Imogen's shocked reaction and hurried on . . . "A job's a job, I'll never get one here".

"Nonsense, Christo. It's we old 'uns who need to sail away. You stay home, you're young, you shove hard with your oar and no new wave's going to sink you. Australia? Later. For me, now. Who's eating what?'

176

They ate well and danced, Christopher with Cecily.

"Sometimes I think . . ."

"You think what?" she asked.

"Oh, I don't know. You and Basil have seen the best".

"There's best and worst. They keep moving in and out, like a magic lantern focussing. The only thing is we all of us have so little time to bide".

"How long will you be away?"

"Six months if we like it, maybe more. I don't like this music, do you?"

"No" he said.

At the table, the talk went on into late hours.

"So, what do we do about our Chris? Leslie Joyce turned up trumps".

"Yes. Very grateful. I even got a play broadcast".

"I heard. More in the pipeline?"

"He's writing a novel" Imogen said.

"A novel?"

"I'm trying" said Christopher. "I want to write a play, too", quickly . . . "But, in the meantime, there's bread and butter".

"You're a lucky boy".

"Oh?"

"To have so many irons. Acting is for any fool . . ."

"You play the piano".

"When I'm not careful, yes. When I am, I have but one outlet for profit. I depict. One day, perhaps, again, in London, who knows? I mean, they can't go on looking back in anger forever. When they start looking back in pleasure, old Basil will be there. God and the kangaroos permitting. Imogen? Home, then? Cecily, why don't you pay the bill and get me out of here?"

It was in the summer that he met Claire Walker again. She telephoned and came to tea. Imogen had gone north for a few days to talk business with her father and Claire had come south for shopping. And had telephoned.

"There's been quite a change here" she said.

"Imogen has transformed it beyond recognition" said

177

Christopher and showed his flat with pride, described the alterations.

"You haven't seen the building since?" he asked.

"No".

"Would you like to see Imogen's flat? I'm sure she would want you to".

"I'd love it. The housekeeper has a key?"

"I . . . have one".

Claire Walker admired the planning and achievement of her daughter and they descended, again, to Christopher's abode.

"I do love coming to London. But I only manage it once in a blue moon".

"Does Mr. Walker bring you down?"

"Sam never travels south if he can possibly avoid it. But I love to shop".

"What a pity Imogen isn't here" he said.

"Yes. Who did that painting?"

"My mother".

"Really? It's very good. It expresses a longing. doesn't it? To escape?"

"Yes".

"I though I'd see a show or two while I'm here. What do you recommend?"

"It's quite a question. They're rather a dull lot of plays, I'm afraid. Unless you like gloom?"

"Hate it. What about a musical?"

He produced a newspaper and ran a finger down the theatre column.

"There's one at the Fortune" he said. "It's called *At the Drop of a Hat*".

"That sounds like us. You will come with me?"

She paid for the tickets, Sam had an account with the agency, she said.

After the theatre, they went to the little club—Christopher had become a member—and he gave her a slap-up meal.

"I like it here" she said. "Won't you ask me to dance?"

He did. He was excited to hold her in his arms. She was so like her daughter but there was a warmth added by maturity—she was, he supposed, forty something, not much. The scent she used lifted him into a world he had not known as yet. A world of calmer, surer reaction by the senses. Of unsudden but deeper thrill. Of 'hot ice and wondrous strange snow', as old Theseus had said of the 'rude mechanicals'.

He wondered if Claire, too, felt excitement at the nearness but she gave no clue at all. A graceful dancer, giving with her body but never without control. She smiled, catching his eye, and for a moment their cheeks touched. Christopher could never fall in with the American form which allowed a moist male stranger to rub facial skin with a female who, surely, had spent time and care on the preparation of hers. Moreover, as now for instance, the momentary brush could mean so much more.

"Shall we sit down?"

Christopher saw that she was able to destroy the concentration of every man in the room. A beautiful walk she had, he noticed as he followed her proudly to the table.

In the spring, Christopher was offered an engagement with a new repertory company that was to operate in a Yorkshire town not far from Leeds.

"The experience is just what I need" he said to Imogen. "It won't be forever" he added, to excuse the relief in his voice.

"What about your book?"

"It's been hanging fire. Maybe a new environment will help that too . . ." Only now did he see, fully, the pain his clumsy blurtings had caused. The realisation went further, too, to light up the true reason for his eagerness. A fillip to his career, yes. He might have included the ability to pay his own way but he left this dark corner unillumined. Reluctant as he was to admit that the sickness still recurred, his main concern was to be on his amatory way. The battered hat of his integrity had been brushed and handshaped to forbid his playing the physical field. While under Imogen's roof he was able to conform to an uneasy standard, not even Jackie revisited again. But the hat was too far gone for reblocking. He needed the break now. The break away in order to break out. Yes. She no longer attracts you, you know how to treat it, you've had it often enough, keep taking the tablets.

The green eyes had filled with tears. They didn't pierce like her father's but he suspected they did their reading of him.

"You . . . won't be all that far from home. My home. I might go north to stay for a while, I could drive over and see you".

"That'd be super" he said.

The book closed with too loud a click together, leaving much of her imprisoned in uncut pages.

Imogen packed his belongings for travelling and taxied him to the station.

In the fifth week of the season—he was playing Branwell Brontë with the self indulgence that never does make up for too quick learning under sloppy direction—a knock came on his dressing room door.

"A Miss Walker to see you" said the pimply girl A.S.M.

Christopher was standing at a cracked wash basin, wearing only a jock strap which revealed much by leaving the back uncovered, more by covering the front. He had the luxury of dressing alone but the room was used for storing props too and a certain amount of coming and going—mostly by females—went with the privilege of isolation. He was drying his face with a towel, using the last clean patch.

"Imogen!"

The towel was still, momentarily, before his eyes. "Sit down, darling, be with you".

He had plunged at once into work after leaving London, finding the activity, like cold water, refreshing and restorative. Manhood, so treated, had begun to return from latency and the blood pulsed unthickened by richness. There wasn't a female worth a damn within distance though, and the vision of Imogen the comforter was attractive anew.

"'Tisn't Imogen" said a voice.

180

Claire had a way with speech that he entirely approved. She stamped it gently, firmly, 'Claire'. Affectation it could be called and, in a sense, was. An aristocratic edge to the tone and a perfection, absolute, to the sounding of the vowels. Imogen's speaking was warmer but he found the pure ice of Claire irresistible.

"Mrs. Walker, she said. 'Miss'. I say, do forgive me".

She stood by the closed door and looked at him with clear blue eyes that told nothing. Nothing but beauty. He was conscious of being nearly naked and of becoming more so by the moment.

"Do, please . . . I . . ." He fell silent and returned her gaze.

She made no effort to leave the room, nor to turn, nor even to stop looking. A smile puckered her lips and they parted at last. He smiled back as he grabbed at his robe, on a hook nearby. It was a present from Imogen.

CHAPTER

22

Christopher sat in a corner of the Station Hotel lounge. A sudden shaft of sunlight startled the dust and soot that had hung in the air unseen, only felt. The lounge, at that hour, was not too busy a thoroughfare and such a hotel, being on a railway station, is not too great a deflection in one's aimed journey from A to B.

He had an hour to kill. A point which made him ponder, at once, the ease with which he had made greater killings. The years following his final leave-taking of Imogen were a battlefield of hopeful youngsters hacked to death. By the time you learn to live with the years, he thought, they were old enough—as Rex would be one day—to kick hope and you into the ash-can.

181

"Coffee?"

No 'sir'? No, sir, not any more. The revolution had been bloodless but complete. Everybody equal, nobody happy. Christopher declined and the waiter scowled and walked away. He doubted whether the man had the power to eject a sitter not drinking or doing something to bring profit to B.R. He was certain he would like to have it. He was equally certain that the profit to B.R. wouldn't enter into it, wouldn't get a foot in the doorway. Dangerous, in this day, to be a mere subject in plain clothes at the mercy of even half a uniform. What is it attracts a man—or a woman—to the wearing of a uniform?

An hour to kill, before he put his manuscript into the hands of the publisher. He would telephone Jenny. She was expecting that he would stay overnight in London—"Late talks, dinner at the Club, can't rush these things . . ."—but he would telephone her. To allay suspicion.

He looked again at the dancing smut in the air and recalled another hotel. Before the battle with the years had been joined . . .

'I'm in Leeds for a few days and Imogen said I must come over to see you".

Imogen said. He pulled the robe more tightly about him and set a chair for Claire.

"How is she?"

"I gather you don't write very often . . ?"

"I . . . You work night and day here".

"Weekends too? Tomorrow?"

"Sundays I study".

"Pity".

"Why?"

She used the minimum of words and he dropped into step with her. "I was going to suggest we go for a drive, talk about things".

"I'd love to".

She smiled but not unkindly. As though remembering back to young behaviour. "What about your study?"

"Next week we're playing *Lady in the Sun* . . ."

182

"You're old part?"

"No. Basil Smart's. But I know it backwards".

"I'll drive over and pick you up, then. About eleven?"

"Fine".

There was a hesitation between them. Then she said . . . "I'd better drive you home now, see where you live. Unless you have a date?"

"A date, no . . . Thank you".

A further hesitation, he began to take off the robe.

"I'll wait outside" she said.

The hotel in Leeds was very different from the one in which a decade and a half later, he would remember. Claire commanded respect and something more, he noticed. Sam Walker would be known here, his money would buy even respect, but Christopher knew that if she had been Claire Anyone Else the deference would be as marked. As they entered, he thought it must be like this to walk beside a princess. The revolution would not dare to touch Claire, she would be the one whose appearance would silence the crowd.

As he sat opposite her in the ornate restaurant, he felt like a schoolboy being fêted at half-term. By a very young mother. Old enough, just old enough. But young. Her eyes were bright, her skin smooth and glowing. She must use make-up, of course, but he couldn't detect more than a suggestion of it. The young girls he had known, even Imogen, could take lessons from her. In the use of make-up and in the preservation of self that would lessen the need for it. Why was it young girls, most of them, looked older than Claire? No, they didn't, this was nonsense. But he thought of Jackie and of Liane whose excesses left deep marks. A few days in the fresh air, a few nights devoted to sleep . . . and youth renews itself. He looked again at Claire. How long did the renewal continue, he wondered. He looked at his own reflection in the mirrored wall behind her and laughed aloud at the dark shadows beneath his eyes. Claire had none.

"Why are you laughing?"

"I caught sight of myself in the glass. I look awful."

"Working night and day?" she said. And they both laughed.

They had coffee in her sitting-room and took cigarettes from her gold case. As he put forward the flame of his lighter, their fingers touched, momentarily. Hers were pink-nailed, feminine, uncertain. He began, yet again, to assess the differences between mother and daughter. Imogen had her father's assurance, the arrogance of it tempered by a little inherited femininity from Claire. The assurance of Claire was a quality of the stock and was unneeding of emphasis. So that she was able to command and yet be feminine to a degree not attainable by Imogen. He was conscious again, but barely, of the presence of scent.

She exhaled the smoke and he glimpsed her clear, pink tongue against the white, very white teeth. He realised that he had been alarmed about these, they had seemed to be too well made for nature. His relief, now, alarmed him more. She had thrown back her head and the translucence had told him the truth. The delicate tone of the lip colouring, the eyelashes—long and natural, the groomed chestnut hair . . . As though conscious of his scrutiny, she rose and moved away. He was able to notice again the slim legs, the smallness of the feet, expensively enclosed. Everything about her clothing had the unobtrusive, casual rightness only money can achieve. Money and instinct in choice. She wore a mulberry coloured suit of tweed but not tweed, Christopher didn't know what the hell it was, only that the jacket hung like the only jacket he possessed that hung at all. Was it cut by Sam's tailor? The thought created a ludicrous nearness between them. Hers was cut to lay the merest of stresses on that very narrow waist—she had passed this, fully, with the measure of femininity, to Imogen. A thoroughbred to watch in motion as she walked away from him. The length of leg he guessed easily, the small buttocks so clearly not encased in those damned elastic affairs that made rigid the middles and lowers of most women of her age. My God, she could—had he permitted life to lead him—have been his mother-in-law and here he was, wanting to possess her! He laughed, lightly but aloud, at the thought. Claire turned.

184

"What now?"

"Just . . . thought. I've had such a good time, thank you".

"'Tisn't over yet".

She faced him fully and he was sure that the pink of her cheeks had deepened. Imperceptibly. But he perceived.

"How is your book?" she asked casually.

"Book?"

"The novel you're writing. Or aren't you?"

"In fits and starts. I don't know how the hell . . ." He paused, wondering whether one said things like this to one's elders. However gorgeous. She wore tiny gold earrings and something gold at her throat. A ropey necklet of some kind, just seen. A shirt, it was, a kind of silk shirt under the jacket which was cut like a cardigan, no lapels.

"How the hell, what?"

"Writers. I don't know how the hell they live. I wouldn't mind sitting back and having a go at a book but who pays the rent?" It was his turn to colour up. Very perceptibly.

"My daughter, surely? I thought that was established, she is your patron. That's what she told me and her father".

"I know".

"Both Sam and Imogen share this fixed idea that they have a responsibility".

"To the Arts?"

"To the Arts and to individuals. Of course, when it comes to individuals, a different kind of response to responsibility may be involved. Imogen is in love with you. Even if she weren't, she would want to help you in your book but, being in love with you, she will expect responses. If we accept patronage we must earn it, you and I. I by being what I am and—in Sam's view—worthy of preservation . . ." Her eyes laughed now . . . "You by your work. The love angle is something else again. If we accept love because comfort goes with it . . . we must give, at least, loyalty in return". She seemed to be answering something in his look when she added: "Unfailing loyalty. Don't you feel?"

"Which brings me back . . ." he said ". . . to who pays the rent".

"So you're not in love?" Then, sadly . . . "If you are, it doesn't matter a damn which of you has money".

"I'm very fond of Imogen".

"That doesn't answer. Or, rather, it does. Completely. You're pulling out, then?"

"Yes. I'm sorry".

"Why? I would like to pull out myself sometimes".

He looked at her in blank astonishment. She smiled to confirm that what she had said was the truth and that she was accustomed to tell it. He supposed, even, that she would be as open with Sam or, in behaviour, refuse at least to be openly hypocritical.

"You're not in love either?"

"I never pretended to be more than, as you say, fond. Did you pretend?" The directness took him off balance. "Of course you did" she said, "Men do. When they need to".

A shaft of June sunlight came into the room and lit the atomies in the air.

"I planned a picnic until I saw how ghastly the day was. It's clearing up. Shall we go for a drive?"

He drove the noiseless Bentley at her request and knew what it was to be in power. She sat, turned more than a little towards him, her arm resting on the back of her seat, he could see the hand out of the corner of his eye, the spread, tentative fingers.

The merest touch of the accelerator brought response. They overtook the last of the Leeds traffic.

"Gently, Christopher. We have all afternoon".

"I didn't realise. I've never driven a car like this before".

'Christopher'. He had never heard it sound so like music.

They were soon in countryside and she directed him to a lane that led to another lane and then to isolation. Trees and green, untrodden grass. The sunlight coming, again, on cue. They stood looking into a clear, unhurried stream and the wind lifted her hair. The back of her neck, so revealed, she seemed to sense as a nakedness and she drew away, avoiding his eyes. They crossed the stream by a narrow bridge and climbed a low, easy slope to an elm that had been there always. Huge, spreading. They sat beneath it and the wind lifted the skirt of her hair again. The sound

186

of a plane, circling, seemed to menace them, looking up together they saw the black dot scrawling the sky with a chalk of white. The kiss happened and she gave a little moan of mingled protest and relief as she lay back, drinking from him, as from a spring long denied. The mouth was soft, giving, taking. The lips trembled as he drew back from her, because there was naked love on his face, in his eyes.

"No use . . ." she said, "telling you we shouldn't".

"I love you, Claire".

"You mean you want me".

"I want you too, but I love you".

"You want me" she said. But, to herself. "You want me", and their mouths were open again to one another. His fingers undid the jacket without lapels, explored beneath it, grasped her breasts, pulled the shirt up from the skirt, went under the looseness, touched her body at last.

"Christopher".

His hands were behind her and, in a moment, they slipped round to the front of her body, lifted away her clothing. Away and up. His hands grasped her shoulders and the bra and shirt lay tightly across his wrists as he held her from him, looked at her.

"Do you take everything you want? Like this?" She lay below him, nearly naked to the waist, her breasts fuller than her daughter's, but firm still and young, strangely young. As though time, in respect too, had forborne to take toll, had waited, with her, for a last fullness in loving.

She made no protest as he took off the jacket, the shirt, the bra. The gold necklet and earrings underlining her nakedness, she lay, unprotesting, her heart beating fast, her skin aglow. But unprotesting. He remembered his revelation of Imogen and the horror in her eyes. In the eyes of Claire, there was only resignation. He opened his shirt and held her to him, skin to skin.

"Claire".

"Yes?"

"I love you".

"Don't. Don't pretend with me. Take me but don't pretend".

"It isn't . . . I'm not. I've never said it to anyone. 'I love you,' I mean".

"That means you want me more, that's nice".

"Don't you? Want me?"

"Yes. Sinful, isn't it?"

"I don't think so".

"Then you don't know what sin is. I'll tell you what sin is, it's wanting. You don't have to do, if you want to do, that's sin".

The thickness of her bunched skirt cushioned her a little from the ground. He left her only the skirt and the half slip and the tiny suspender belt. The stockings that had clothed her long legs so elegantly in silk were about her ankles, her expensive shoes still on her feet. So that her degradation, as she lay panting and open to him, was as complete as the moment he called 'love'.

CHAPTER

23

He ordered his fourth large brandy. The Station Hotel waiter was no happier than he had been at the first refusal, poor British Rail. These are surly days, old Chris. The trick is to stand out against the day and age, to hang on to your slow old values, not to get caught in the slipstream. But you did, didn't you? A bit young, the values hadn't had time to set firm? Maybe. The sun lit the atomies again. They had been clear in the Leeds sitting-room of Claire but they had dirtied up.

"Christopher, as I live and choke!"

Through a rising mist of British Rail alcohol, he saw a distorted but familiar face.

"Basil!"

"By Christ, 'he's pissed too". Basil looked at his watch.
"And the sun isn't even half way up the fo'c'sle". He smelled
what remained of the contents of the glass. "Brandy.
Waiter!"

He sat opposite Christopher, pulling the chair close to
the low, solid table that stood between them.

"What are you doing here, drowning 'em?"

"Drowning 'em" said Christopher. "What are you?"

"Off to Rome to appear in a motion picture. Something
quite new. Nobody undresses".

"I thought you wouldn't be speaking to me".

"I'm not. That's to say, a good deal of soda has splashed
into the alc. since those days. Didn't care for the book".

"Nor did I".

"Old Paul and I decided, nem. con., that you were a
Tom Tit".

"I was. I still am".

"Ah . . . Oh, waiter . . . a large brandy and soda . . ."

"Two".

"All right, two. Heard you got married".

"On the proceeds of the book, how's that".

"L.B.W. What's she like? From the roseate view I had of
you in days of yore, I'd say she must be quite something
to turn you into what she turned you into".

"She didn't, I did. How's Cecily?"

"In form. Bit delicate, we have to watch the old lady.
But we do. Why don't you give her a call, she's on her
own for a whole month and even she may have got over
you by now".

"Thanks".

"No offence, old crusader, but you really did set up a
bit of an aroma. They made a talking film too, of sorts.
We began to think Paul would never live down that little
matter of falling for that little matter".

"I'm sorry. I can't bloody well say more. If you want
to . . ."

"Steady on! Drunk is all right but fighting drunk, no.
Just a splash for me, fill his right up" he said to the waiter.
Christopher accepted the bid to ration him.

"Surly days" 'he said.

"Come?"

"You're going white, Mr. Smart".

"A wonder I have any hair left at all, the way the world keeps chopping at our fundamentals. Picture of your wife?"

" 'Mm?"

"A picture, I said. Of your wife, like to see it, you have one?"

What had really attracted him to little Jenny Frühling was the complete newness of her. The newness and the cleanness. On that night of champagne, all had been Christmas and discovery. At first light they made vows, at second they consummated for the second time with consummate care. In the opening of this, the most precious package, he could not be without it. Jenny wasn't on any pill and he had, once only— on a signal occasion, neglected to use his infallible, all time great little what'sit. The jelly bit he had evolved a great technique with, they never knew, they always wondered. But he, no. "I'm sterile" he used to say to them with a serious pan, knowing that all was well by hook or by science. The little sixteen-year-old had answered, with just as serious a pan "Does that mean you can't . . . ? But you are!

His flat-mate had offered to move out when they would get wed—not long now, Christopher had told Jenny, scratching and tapping away at the novel. Having met Jenny, the flat-mate suggested he might move back later, as a lodger? Help out with the rent? No, said Christopher and offered to let him have the flat. No, he said. Jenny worked, he worked, and then he met a man with a film set-up who read the story so far and bought it.

They married at St. Marylebone Register Office on Jenny's twenty first.

"I love you" she mouthed to him soundlessly as the little man read the words. He mouthed back "I love you too". Then he faced front, looking at the ceiling.

"You mean you want me" a voice said to him. Christopher looked about him, then at the little man, then at

Jenny, it couldn't be Jenny. She was smiling up, happy, trusting. She had just become his wife.

As they signed, he knew that he could never tell Jenny about that signal occasion.

"Of course I have a picture. Every man has a wife of his picture".

"Prove it".

"Prove it, prove it . . ." Christopher began to mutter as his hand moved smudgily from one pocket to another. "Nobody believes me, nobody believes in me, I'm singled out for disbelief. Prove it. WHY SHOULD I HAVE TO PROVE IT?"

"You don't. Shut up".

Basil looked to the far end of the lounge and saw that the waiter was eyeing them with some pleasure.

"We'll get thrown out" he said quietly.

"Let us. Let 'em. She's beautiful, you'll see. When I . . ."

"What's her name?"

"Jenny. Jenny! There she is". He produced a photograph from his wallet and waved it defiantly at Basil.

Basil held his wrist to steady the picture, then took it from him. "Who's the baby?"

"Who's the baby, what do you mean who's the baby, it's my baby".

"I thought it might be. What gender?"

"Mas . . . masculine. It's a he. A son".

"Ah. Called?"

"Rex".

"Splendid. You look better in the picture than you do now, I will say. And Jenny looks as though she wouldn't know how many people you carved up in that book."

"She didn't".

"Happily married, I trust?"

"Could be".

"What do you mean, 'could be'?"

"Just . . . something happened when the kid happened".

"You talk about him as though he were somebody else's. Is he?"

191

"Bastard. You, I mean. Of course he isn't. Is. **Mine**".

"What happened when Rex happened?"

"Poor Jenny. Too much alone. I racket around, try to make money. 'Sponsibilities. Too much alone. Then we moved to Tagham . . ."

"Where the hell's that?"

"Sussex. Heart of. In. Furnished cottage. They have this drama society in the next town. And thereby hangs something else. My fault".

"What is?"

"I made her join".

"You make her act with amateurs?"

"Yes".

"Poor Jenny".

"Poor Jenny, what do you mean 'poor Jenny'?"

"Quiet. Go on, though".

"I thought it would be nice for her to have an outlet. Now she's got an inlet. He's younger than I am, nobody isn't. Except you. And he isn't a Tom Tit. Except he is. If he takes my Jenny, he is".

"Who is?"

"Leading amateur. Means lover, you know".

"I know. You mean he hasn't yet?"

"If she wants him, she can bloody well have him, don't you misunderstand me".

"I don't".

"Never ran after a woman. Ever".

"She's your wife!"

"And don't you forget it".

Something happened when Rex happened, Jenny thought. Maybe I get too absorbed, anyone gets absorbed when they have Rex. Can't remember when we last went to bed. That way, I mean. He was absorbed too, at first. He used to bath Rex. And then he started looking at me as though I were a stranger. Not a stranger person but a stranger piece of cattle. Kept asking was I doing my exercises. I caught him looking at me on the sly whenever I stripped. Tummy like a bag of jelly, everybody's tummy is like a bag of jelly after you've had Rex. It goes down, mine went down. I caught him looking at my breasts, too, as if he were just looking at somebody's breasts, sizing them up. They're my breasts and he always said they were breasts to cherish. Hell, when you feed Rex . . . Anyway, they snapped right back to what they were, like my tummy, a little bit fuller though, which is nice. My breasts, not my tummy . . .

"Ever have any Rexes?"

"No. It didn't happen. Cecily can't now, why?"

"You're lucky".

"We don't think so".

"They take over. Like a dise-e-ease . . ."

He drew the word out and a stout lady opposite him got up. Basil turned his head and met her stare with innocence. She left, though.

"A disease!"

"I heard you" said Basil, looking back at him again.

"A creeping disease. Before you can say 'knife' . . . What does that mean, who wants to say 'knife'?"

"Go on about the disease".

"I don't want to say 'knife', do you?"

"Not often".

"Marriage comes out in spots. All over. Every time you . . . you know . . . want to . . . you know . . ."

"Yes?"

"There's a bloody great bellow from the next room and up she rises. No 'hurray', though, just up she rises. And down go you. If you follow?"

"I follow".

"After a while, you don't even bother to come up because you're waiting for it. That bellow. So's she. Ruins your sex life. When you lie there with both ears cocked, there isn't going to be anything much else cocked, believe you me. Not ever again. S'pity".

"Why don't you get a girl in?"

"To sleep with, you mean?"

"No. To look after Rex".

N

"What do we pay her with?"

"Things that bad?"

"They're not that good. S'awful. Patho . . . psycho . . . S'awful".

"What is?"

"Started when I couldn't look at her little . . . you know . . . they're pretty one's too . . . without remembering he'd just finished eating 'em".

"Shut up".

"Shut up, yes. S'have a drink".

"One more for you, you'll spill it out of the top of your head".

"S'have a drink. Waiter!"

It was Christopher suggested we move to Tagham. The cottage was going cheap and it's a quiet place for writing. Rex does cry a lot but he's teething, after all, and now Chris uses the boxroom. To sleep in. Or type in, he's been typing half the night, a new novel I think. The last one made quite a bit but since we got married it's been mostly radio plays—and a couple of television half-hours, they get him in when the chief writers on the series run out of ideas. He wrote himself a part in the first one but he hasn't done it since, he thinks they don't like it. I told him what the hell, he was good. He said yes but so are too many others, he must stick to what he thinks he might be able to do better than some. I think he sets store by this book. What's 'good', anyway, I begin to think people don't know any more. I'm good but the best part I ever had was with that bloody choc-bar.

Chris's father is loaded, or he's married to a loaded lady but there's no help there. His foster-father left him a couple of thousand which really pulled us out of the you know what but it made Chris miserable as hell. I couldn't make him out, I mean they were very sweet people, I met them often, but they'd had a good life and everybody dies and if they do it leaving you something to remember them by, something like two thousand, I'd think you might be like pleased. He didn't speak for days.

194

Then he made this suggestion about my joining the drama group. If there's one thing I can't stand it's amateurs but he said it would be good for me and I could take Rex too, leave him with the director's wife during rehearsals, she hasn't got any and dotes on anyone else's. I agreed because I thought it would give Chris time to himself. Time away from me. Then he took to going up to London twice a week. To sniff around, he said. Well, tonight he's spending the night, his first ever away from me. Sniffing around. If you ask me, he's got somebody. Who's crying? I never felt less like crying in my life because that's perfectly all right, because so have I.

He's younger than I am.

We're doing the Prime of Jean Brodie and the silly thing is he's playing the schoolmaster—he's miles too young . . . and I'm playing the schoolgirl. After all's said and done, though, I'm very slight and I look years younger than I am. When I told Chris they'd offered me the part I thought at least he'd show a bit of interest. I mean, it was his idea my joining this group of weirdies, you'd think he'd be ever so slightly fascinated they'd offered me this part. He was correcting some typescript and it took him all of half a minute to even answer.

"Good" was what he said when he did.

"Do you think it's all right?"

"Of course, why?"

"I have to strip naked, there's a scene where he's painting my picture".

He actually looked up. "Really? Surely, with amateurs, they'll cut that bit?"

That got me on the raw, that really got me on the raw. He makes me join, now he's knocking them. I was very cool.

""You can't. Do you think it's all right?"

"What will the vicar's wife say?"

I nearly came out with a four letter word, I don't make a practice of coming out with them. "I don't give a . . . damn about the vicar's wife, I'm asking you." So 'damn' is a four letter word, I meant the other one. "Is it all right?"

195

"For you to strip? Depends. Your figure's pretty well back to normal, isn't it?"

Well. I just didn't utter, I didn't utter. I stomped out of the room and went upstairs and cried my eyes out. Yes, all right, I know.

Of course, I accepted the part. I wasn't that keen to show the village my bottom but I was fucked if I was going to let Chris patronise me. Yes, I know. It was a marvellous part—though the cast is pretty crappy, they always are. And after working in the professional theatre, I found everything and everybody drove me up the wall.

"Now, we must get down to learning our words" said the director. 'Words'! I mean, that sent me, that really sent me, I fell about inside because, of course, I call them 'lines'.

Then came the time when he took John and me aside at rehearsal. John is playing the schoolmaster.

"Tomorrow night", he said, "I'll take your scene, just the two of you. There won't be any prying eyes so, Jenny, if you'll . . . bring along a bathing suit or something . . ." A professional director would have said "Come prepared to strip off and let's get on with it", but not Cyril. He coloured up to the roots. John smiled at me and I back at him. We were beginning to have this rapport.

I did bring a bathing suit, for a laugh. Then I helped Cyril out.

"I think I'd better strip right off and get used to the feeling, don't you?"

"Fine, yes".

When I felt John's eyes on me, his glance moving up and down my body, I got the shock of my life. I mean, he has to do that, he's supposed to be painting me but wow! I said everything and everybody in this set-up drove me up the wall, that was a form of expression. Lying naked in front of John and being looked at—to hell with Cyril, he was queer and didn't know it anyway—something else was driving me up the wall. Just plain old desire.

It brought to mind that first evening with Christopher. Evening, what do I mean, 'evening'—night. Champagne we had. That was a first, too. I undressed in the bedroom but the door was ajar. You know how it is with shadows and light, I don't know. I undressed. Then, all at once, I knew he'd been watching me. Or my shadow, what? In one big moment-all-to-myself, I got the once only thrill a girl gets when she shows herself to a man for the first time. Now, I was showing myself again. For the second time and not to Christopher and yet it must have been to Christopher really or how do you account for that whoops?

"Let's run the scene again" Cyril said.

Again, oh boy. Oh boy, oh boy.

"That's enough" gasped Christopher, "I'm all right now".

Basil turned off the tap and allowed Christopher to ease his head from under it. He gave him a towel.

"I . . . don't know what happened".

"You got pissed, that's what happened. Mid-morning is a bit early. I have just half an hour before my train leaves, I suggest we wrap ourselves round a gallon of coffee".

"Wrap me round, you mean".

"Whatever you say".

"What became of that nice Imogen you were doing? I thought you were rather all set with her".

"She was loaded".

"So were you until I shoved you under the cold tap".

"Money, I mean".

"That old thing".

Coffee arrived and the waiter snorted to prove something. He didn't.

"Don't like to be bought".

"Agree. I don't like to be sold, nor does P. Bannerman".

"Oh Christ, are we back to that?"

"Just . . . trying to sort you out".

"Sort me out. This . . . "—he took up his spring-back that enclosed the novel—" . . . will sort me out".

"Another book?"

"Another book".

"Autobiography of a Tom Tit?"

Christopher swallowed half a cup of coffee before he answered. "You could say".

"Any mention of Imogen?"

"Not by name".

"By other names we smell as high. Jackie. Liane?"

"Yes".

"Me?"

"Yes again".

"I thank you. Paul, I suppose, in passing?"

"In passing".

"You're a Tom Tit".

"That's what you said this was the autobiography of".

"Jenny?"

"Come?'

"Jenny? Mention of Jenny?"

"But of course".

"I . . . don't think I shall buy it".

"Others may. I hope. If they don't, I don't pay the cottage rent. Or buy the cottage cheese, even".

"So. For you to eat bread, your friends eat dirt?"

"Know who made me write *Some Defect in Her*?"

"Who?"

"That nice Imogen. She said the work justified the crucifixion".

"She was taking you for a genius, you're no genius, you're just a Tom Tit. Why don't you throw that away and go and see my agent?"

"Throw what away? This?"

"This, that. I have this agent. Come to think of it, he's a Tom Tit. Stops at nothing to get work for me. What he couldn't do for a Tom Tit, imagine!"

198

Christopher was silent, Basil scribbled on a card. "You used to be an actor, you had promise" he was saying. "You could have it again. Now that the new wave is old hat and folk are laughing once more, albeit hysterically, why not get in there? And stop pitching against your friends?"

"I have no friends".

"Ta-ta-tee" sang Basil, to the tune of Hearts and Flowers and mimed the playing of a fiddle. "Got a wife, haven't you? Stop pitching against her, then. Just pitch".

John suggested it. Or was it Cyril, I think it might have been Cyril. And John took it up. About rehearsing privately.

"Don't have to do it in the nude, Mrs. Tighson". I have to tell you that, in addition to not knowing he's a poof, he doesn't know he's not a comedian, either. And 'Mrs. Tighson', for Christ's sake we'd been working together for weeks. Do you *know* how long amateurs rehearse?

Christopher came out with about staying overnight in London—with his popsie or whatever . . . I said to John "Come on over, we'll rehearse".

I asked Christopher, of course. I think it was to allay suspicion, really, I had mentioned John once or twice—in defence of the weirdies, said he was good. And good looking. If you think it got a response, you don't know matrimony that has gone so stale there are green, live what the hell do they call them, cultures—that's a laugh, that name is —all over it. Chris hadn't a suspicion in that beautiful head. If he'd loved me, he would have had, I mean, for Christ's sake, I was showing my all in this drama. To this John. Nothing.

I said goodbye to Christopher at eight forty, he was in a hurry to get the train. He had his novel under his arm, I hadn't read a word of it, or heard a word of it—he used to read me everything he wrote. So, it was his novel. And he said there might be late talks, he couldn't rush them. I wonder what she's like. Thank God he doesn't know to wonder what mine is like. John, I mean.

Well, I knew, and if my husband didn't want me any more, he did, we had this rapport. Not a word had passed,

199

you understand, only the words in the play. But a woman knows.

I made it the afternoon, Rex sleeps in the afternoon. If this worked out, this clandestine bit—I know the word because there's this play I played in at Drama School called *The Clandestine Marriage*, 'clandestine' means secret. Only it sounds grander. And wickeder . . . If this clandestine bit worked out, I'd get a nanny. We couldn't afford one but I'd sell my Marks and Spencer shares that I bought from sucking the choc-bar on T.V.—they'd gone up, if you'll excuse the phrase they're always going up—and I'd get one. Not for Christopher. But so's I could make clandestine assignations with John and Rex wouldn't start bawling. I'd have an understanding with the nanny. On days when my gentleman friend was set to call, she'd gag Rex with Sellotape. What am I saying, she'd take him out, I mean! Does everybody who has Rex stop having sex, God!

He came for tea. Only we didn't wait, we went straight into our scene. From the play. Now, of course, I was fully clothed but the memory of not having been clothed at all last week when we did it made me colour up and whoops. He did, too. A bit. He's handsome in a young, dolly sort of way. And I kept trying to imagine he was as handsome as my Chris in the days when my Chris was as handsome as John and still wanted me.

'You're crying" John said.

"No, I'm not" I said.

"Well, I'm on the outside, looking, and I'd say like anything you're crying".

"Just because a person has tears in her eyes, it doesn't automatically follow" I said. I didn't know what the hell I meant either but I thought blind him with maturity. Then he acted as though I was crying, which of course I was and he put his arms round me.

"Darling!"

"You're not supposed to say that".

"We're not rehearsing now".

"We are. We must be".

"We're not" he said and he was quite what you'd call masterful.

"The kettle's whistling" I said, which, as a matter of fact, it was.

"I don't give a bugger" he said. Then, "I say, I'm terribly sorry".

"What for?"

"Saying 'bugger' ".

"What you mean to say is you're not keen on tea?"

'No. Kiss me, Jenny".

Kiss him, what did he mean, kiss him, men kiss girls. I think he sensed this because he did.

Upstairs, it was all a bit clinical. He was beautiful, naked, he'd seen me naked already so I don't suppose I rated. But he did. I thought of my Chris and the night he'd stood there in the bedroom of that flat he shared with what-was-his-name, old Adam and Eve and lech me . . . I was standing there, actually, when Chris came in.

"You're beautiful, little Jenny" he said.

"So are you" I said, "but you're overdressed".

Then he undressed in front of me until the two of us were naked. It was a great moment.

John stood there and I stood there and it seemed I had to take all the initiative. In the end, somehow, we found ourselves on the bed and I felt a sodding great whoops of remorse or something. After all it was our bed. I mean, the least John could do would be to get very excited and be all over me, so to speak. You'd think. It took him quite a time. And little active things Christopher had taught me I had to resort to. It occurred to me I hadn't resorted to them with Christopher in ages. Christopher was always so active I'd got into the way of being passive. So I was active.

John held me in his arms and I was shamed out of my mind by this fact that the only way I could thrill myself was to close my eyes and remember Christopher. John was a poor shadow and I was doing all the work. I wondered suddenly whether it would have been better if, with Chris, I had done at least some of it some of the time.

Then it happened. No, not that, listen. Beautiful John—and he was beautiful, he made me think a lot of Chris—was lying there atop his schoolgirl—and I'm pretty beautiful too, I'm no physical slouch—and things were starting to go according to nature's awful plan . . . when the doorbell went.

"Fuck" he said. Well, you couldn't blame him, he had it pretty much in mind.

There is this drawback about living in the country, people are inclined to drop in. I suppose it isn't the done thing to go to bed in the afternoon, but then you could be having a sleep. He tiptoed to the window, I don't know why, he was stark naked, he wouldn't have made any noise. I took a sly look at his bottom, it was firm and small. Like my Chris's, in so far as I remember. He peered out through the curtain, then looked back over his shoulder with a face like a little boy who'd been caught stealing the jam.

"Mother of God" he said, and his voice had gone up two octaves. "It's the vicar!"

Quick curtain. Everybody out for tea and muffins. We never did go back for the second act.

Christopher walked with Basil to the waiting train. Even the station air, soot-laden, did him good. Or did him bad, he wasn't sure, it had an effect, changed the pace.

"Don't forget to call Cecily".

"I will".

"You mean you won't, don't you, I hope?"

"I do. I won't".

"This is me" Basil said and climbed into a carriage. In a moment, he reappeared at a window and made comedy of not being able to get his head through. "These sliding jobs . . . Not made for goodbyes".

"You be seeing Paul?"

"One of these days, who knows?"

"Give him . . . you know".

"I know".

"And thank you. For . . . "

"I know".

"When you come back . . . "

"I have your number. Look, come in for Christ's sake, this is like talking from Sing Sing".

Christopher joined him in the compartment.

"Only one thing I want to add, old Christopher . . . "

"Lecture?"

"Lecture. You saw what happened to the theatre a decade and a half ago?"

"Yes".

"Wonderful great new wave of freedom. Knocked us arsewise. Trouble is . . . freedom—to be freedom—must be disciplined. Could be it applies to the old love life. Think about it. Train's going. Unless you're coming to Italy too, suggest you fuck off. Communicate?"

"Communicate".

Christopher saw the train move away, then moved away himself, back down the platform.

Autobiography of a Tom Tit. He couldn't drop it in the litter bin, it had his name and address on it, he might get it back. But the Thames is a river. And it's so full of muck these days eighty thousand mucky words, parcelled up with a brick, won't notice. Where would he get a brick? Not difficult, they're always pulling down something to put up something else, they'll never—in that sense—finish London.

He passed through the barrier and entered a call box, sorted out his change. He had it in mind to make three calls.

"Book isn't quite right, be in touch with you" put paid to one.

"Love you, Jackie, but won't be seeing you yet awhile" did the second.

Somehow, he didn't want to talk to Jenny in the same breath so he pocketed the rest of the change and walked out of the station.

A movie is a great way of passing the time. While you're plucking up whatever it is you need to pluck up to phone Jenny. At this time of the day nobody's there. But they go through all the motions, the films have been made for the million, they show them. Even to the odd half dozen.

He sat there, darkling, as the Old Bard used to say, meaning in the dark, not hearing a word, seeing a frame. He contemplated the life hitherto of the Tom Tit that was Tighson. The comfort lover.

No comforts any more, this is world without bonuses, amen. No pity, though, for yourself. Leave that to the weaker young. As for you, you want to be free, you bloody well—glaucoma or no glaucoma—do your National Service. For you, Christopher. Learn to slope arms, present and order. Order. In your own private army where the promotion comes strictly from Colonel You.

The unrealities tumbled on the wider than wide screen until, suddenly, there was a pause. Colour slides, telling you of the ten new delights, icie and drinkie, that would come your way—promise!—in a moment. The slids slid and a spotlight splashed on to a spotty girl who thought she was Goldie Hawn. She stands there and you're expected to leave your paid for seat and go down and queue. To pay more money, service with a sneer.

No more comforts, no Goldies. No queueing. He sat slumped in his back stall seat until the spotlight died and Goldie with it. The unrealities began.

It was a film made in England criticising the way the Portuguese run their country. Jesus. He would have like to see a film made in Portugal about the way the British run theirs. They wouldn't make it, though, they're too well mannered.

Close by him walked a pair of long legs that made him think of Jenny. They belonged to another girl with a lighted tray, a small part player, no spotlight. He made a noise that wasn't supposed to sound as though he was summoning her and she came to him with a smile, this is revolution all over again! He asked about the promised goodies but learned that all that stuff on the slides was come-hither.

"There's only Tutti-Frutti".

"No Tutti-Frutti".

"Or orangeade".

"No orangeade".

He settled for a bag of mixed nuts. As she walked away, he remembered something and went to find a telephone.

"Jenny? I'll be home for dinner, change of plan".

"Are you all right?"

"Very much. Little Jenny".

Back in the darkling, he saw a film with stars that had

grace and beauty. Somebody's trying. Trying, hell, they're supplying a demand, hurray for the demand.

Jenny decided to be active. She had to ring John to get Cyril's number. He was sheepish to an amateur degree. She got Cyril.

"Do you think your wife could take Rex? For all night tonight? I'm . . . not going to be here".

"You know she adores him. We never had one of our own, you know . . . " She knew. Had been told. Cyril pattered on . . . "Doris would take him for a year, given the chance".

"She may get it".

Grace and beauty. You may do two things with them Christopher reflected as he watched the now lovely tumble. You may reinstate them when the rot usurps, cherish them, revere them. Or, like the playwrights and others, you may rape them, their stockings to their vulnerable ankles. That too, though, had been productive he had to confess. Claire had borne a son and Sam had been proud, fulfilled.

He thought of Rex. He supposed that sons grew out of bawling and mothers into lovers again.

He opened the plastic bag and felt round for what would come to hand. He resolved, at once, that if it wasn't a Brazil he wouldn't say 'Pity'. Ever again.